When Calls *the* Heart

Books by Janette Oke

*Another Homecoming** *Tomorrow's Dream**
*Return to Harmony**

CANADIAN WEST

When Calls the Heart *When Breaks the Dawn*
When Comes the Spring *When Hope Springs New*
Beyond the Gathering Storm
When Tomorrow Comes

LOVE COMES SOFTLY

Love Comes Softly *Love's Unending Legacy*
Love's Enduring Promise *Love's Unfolding Dream*
Love's Long Journey *Love Takes Wing*
Love's Abiding Joy *Love Finds a Home*

A PRAIRIE LEGACY

The Tender Years *A Quiet Strength*
A Searching Heart *Like Gold Refined*

SEASONS OF THE HEART

Once Upon a Summer *Winter Is Not Forever*
The Winds of Autumn *Spring's Gentle Promise*

SONG OF ACADIA*

The Meeting Place *The Birthright*
The Sacred Shore *The Distant Beacon*
The Beloved Land

WOMEN OF THE WEST

The Calling of Emily Evans *A Bride for Donnigan*
Julia's Last Hope *Heart of the Wilderness*
Roses for Mama *Too Long a Stranger*
A Woman Named Damaris *The Bluebird and the Sparrow*
They Called Her Mrs. Doc *A Gown of Spanish Lace*
The Measure of a Heart *Drums of Change*

Janette Oke: A Heart for the Prairie
Biography of Janette Oke by Laurel Oke Logan

www.janetteoke.com

*with T. Davis Bunn

Canadian West • Book I

When Calls the Heart

Janette Oke

SET

Bethany House Publishers
Minneapolis, Minnesota

When Calls the Heart

Cover design by Jenny Parker

Published by Bethany House Publishers
11400 Hampshire Avenue South
Bloomington, Minnesota 55438

Bethany House Publishers is a division of
Baker Publishing Group, Grand Rapids, Michigan.

Printed in the United States of America

Library of Congress Cataloging-in-Publication Data

Oke, Janette, 1935–
When calls the heart / by Janette Oke.
p. cm. — (Canadian West ; 1)
Summary: "A lovely eastern schoolteacher faces the frontier with the firm resolve to never marry a rowdy adventurer of the West"—Provided by publisher.
ISBN 0-7642-0011-9 (pbk.)
1. Women pioneers—Fiction. 2. Canada, Western—Fiction. I. Title.
II. Series: Oke, Janette, 1935– . Canadian West series ; bk. 1.
PR9199.3.O38W5 2005
813'.54—dc22

2004024206

To my oldest sister,

Elizabeth Margaret (Betty) Cox,

for having the patience
to let me "pull the needle,"
and for many other reasons.

JANETTE OKE was born in Champion, Alberta, to a Canadian prairie farmer and his wife, and she grew up in a large family full of laughter and love. She is a graduate of Mountain View Bible College in Alberta, where she met her husband, Edward, and they were married in May of 1957. After pastoring churches in Indiana and Canada, the Okes spent some years in Calgary, where Edward served in several positions on college faculties while Janette continued her writing. She has written over four dozen novels for adults and children, and her book sales total over twenty-two million copies.

The Okes have three sons and one daughter, all married, and are enjoying their dozen grandchildren. Edward and Janette are active in their local church and make their home near Didsbury, Alberta.

Preface

I would like to supply my readers with a few facts concerning the North West Mounted Police. The Force was founded in 1873 as an answer to the problem of illicit liquor trade and lawlessness in the West. It has been said that the Mountie was dressed in a red coat to readily set him apart from the U.S. Cavalry. The Mountie's job was to make peace with the Indians, not to defeat them; and many of the Indian tribes which he had to deal with had already had run-ins with the troops from south of the border. Whether for this reason, or some other, the scarlet tunic soon became distinctive, and set apart the man who was wearing it.

The uniform and the name both evolved. The title of *Royal* North West Mounted Police was granted by King Edward VII in 1904, in recognition of the Force's contribution to Canada. In 1920, the name was changed to Royal *Canadian* Mounted Police. Eventually, the red coat was adopted as the dress uniform of the Force, and a more practical brown coat was chosen for regular duty, because, said Superintendent Steele, it was "almost impossible for even a neat and tidy man to keep the red coat clean for three months on the trail." The hat also changed from the original pill-box, through various shapes and designs, to the Stetson that was approved in 1901.

It was the Yukon Gold Rush of 1895 that first brought the Mounties into the Far North. By 1898 there were twelve officers and 254 sergeants and constables in the Yukon. The Mounted Police by then were using a new form of transportation—the dog team. With the use of their huskies, they policed hundreds of square miles of snow-covered territory. Trappers, traders and Indian villages were scattered throughout their areas of patrol.

Although I try not to be *too* sentimental when I think of the

Mounties and their part in the development of the Canadian West, to me, they are a living symbol of my Canadian home-land. To the people of the Lacombe area, may I assure you that among the names of Spruceville, Blackfalds, Brookfield, Turville, and Iowalta; Woody Nook, Jones Valley, Canyon, and Eclipse; Eureka, Spring Valley, Arbor Dale, and Blindman; Central, West Branch, Birch Lake, and Lincoln; Milton, Mt. Grove, Sunny Crest, and Morningside; Gull Lake, Lakeside, and Fairview; you will find no Pine Springs. Nor will you find a historic character that matches Pearlie's pa in the town of Lacombe itself. All of the characters in the story are fictional, with no intended likenesses to anyone either living or dead.

May I also assure you that having grown up in the Hoadley area and having spent my early school years in the little one-room school at Harmonien, I have a great deal of love for and many fond memories of rural Alberta community life.

Contents

ONE

Elizabeth

It came as a great surprise to me. Oh, not the letter itself. We were all used to the arrival of letters from brother Jonathan. They came quite regularly and always caused a small stir in our household. No, it wasn't the letter, but rather what it contained that caught me completely off guard. And Mother's response to it was even more astounding.

The day, April 12, 1910, had started out like every other day. I arose early, had a quiet prayer time in my room, cared for my grooming, breakfasted with the family, and left at eight o'clock to walk the eleven blocks to the school where I taught. I had made it a habit to be there early so that I would have plenty of time to make my morning preparations before the students arrived. I was usually the first teacher to make an appearance, but I rather enjoyed the early morning quietness of the otherwise noisy building.

As I walked along on that delightful spring morning, the world appeared especially beautiful and alive. For some reason, the flower-scented air and the song of the birds caused me to take a rare look at my inner self.

And how are you this delightful spring morning? I asked myself.

Why, I am just fine, thank you, I silently answered, and then almost blushed as I quickly looked around for fear that someone might be able to read my thoughts. It wasn't like me to talk to myself—even inwardly, especially when walking along this public, maple-sheltered street. But no one shared the sidewalk with me at the moment so the self-dialogue continued.

Are you now? And what is it that makes your day so glorious—your step so feather-light?

The morning; life itself; the very fragrance of the air I breathe.

'Tis nice—but, then, you have always been a soul who took pleasure in just being alive. I do declare that you would be happy and contented anywhere on God's green earth.

No—not really. Not really.

The sudden turn of the conversation and the switch of my emotion surprised me. There was a strange and unfamiliar stirring deep within me. A restlessness was there, begging me to give it proper notice. I tried to push it back into a recessed corner of my being, but it elbowed its way forward.

You're always doing that! it hotly declared. *Whenever I try to raise my head, you push me down, shove me back. Why are you so afraid to confront me?*

Afraid?

Yes, afraid.

I'm not afraid. It's just that I believe—I've been taught—that one ought to be content with what one has, especially if one has been as blessed as I. It is a shame—no, a sin—to feel discontented while enjoying all of the good things that life—and Papa—have showered upon me.

Aye, t'would be a sin to disregard one's blessings. I should never wish you to do so. But perhaps, just perhaps, it would quiet your soul if you'd look fairly and squarely at what makes the empty little longing tug at you now and then.

It was a challenge; and though I still felt fearful, and perhaps not a little guilty, I decided that I must take a look at this inner longing if the voice was ever to be stilled.

I was born Elizabeth Marie Thatcher on June 3, 1891, the third daughter to Ephraim and Elizabeth Thatcher. My father was a merchantman in the city of Toronto and had done very well for himself and his family. In fact, we were considered part of the upper class, and I was used to all of the material benefits that came with such a station. My father's marriage to my mother was the second one for her. She had first been married to a captain in the King's service. To this union had been born a son, my half-brother, Jonathan.

Mother's first husband had been killed when Jonathan was but three years old; Mother therefore had returned to her own father's house, bringing her small son with her.

My father met my mother at a Christmas dinner given by mutual friends. She had just officially come out of mourning, though she found it difficult to wrap up her grief and lay it aside with her mourning garments. I often wondered just what appealed most to my father, the beauty of the young widow or her obvious need for someone to love and care for her. At any rate, he wooed and won her, and they were married the following November.

The next year my oldest sister, Margaret, was born. Ruthie then followed two years later. Mother lost a baby boy between Ruthie and me, and it nearly broke her heart. I think now that she was disappointed that I wasn't a son, but for some reason I was the one whom she chose to bear her name. Julie arrived two years after me. Then, two and a half years later, much to Mother's delight, another son was born, our baby brother, Matthew. I can't blame Mother for spoiling Matthew, for I know full well that we shared in it equally. From the time that he arrived, we all pampered and fussed over him.

Our home lacked nothing. Papa provided well for us, and Mother spent hours making sure that her girls would grow into ladies. Together my parents assumed the responsibility for our spiritual nurturing and, within the proper boundaries, we were encouraged to be ourselves.

Margaret was the nesting one of the family. She married at eighteen and was perfectly content to give herself completely to making a happy home for her solicitor husband and their little family. Ruth was the musical one, and she was encouraged to develop her talent as a pianist under the tutorship of the finest teachers available. When she met a young and promising violinist in New York and decided that she would rather be his accompanist than a soloist, my parents gave her their blessing.

I was known as the practical one, the one who could always be counted on. It was I whom Mother called if ever there was a calamity or problem when Papa wasn't home, relying on what she referred to as my "cool head" and "quick thinking." Even at an early age I knew that she often depended upon me.

I guess it was my practical side that made me prepare for independence, and with that in mind I took my training to be a teacher. I knew Mother thought that a lady, attractive and pleasant as she had raised me to be, had no need for a career; after all, a suitable marriage was available by just nodding my pretty head at some suitor. But she held her tongue and even encouraged me in my pursuit.

I loved children and entered the classroom with confidence and pleasure. I enjoyed my third-graders immensely.

My sister Julie was our flighty one, the adventure-seeker, the romantic. I loved her dearly, but I often despaired of her silliness. She was dainty and pretty, so she had no trouble getting plenty of male attention; but somehow it never seemed to be enough for her. I prayed daily for Julie.

Matthew! I suppose that I was the only one in the family to feel, at least very often, concern for Matthew. I could see what we all had done to him with our spoiling, and I wondered if we had gone too far. Now a teenager, he was too dear to be made to suffer because of the over-attention of a careless family. He and I often had little private times together when I tried to explain to him the responsibilities of the adult world. At first I felt that my subtle approach was beyond his understanding, but then I began to see a consciousness of the meaning of my words breaking through. He became less demanding, and began to assert himself in the proper sense, to stand independently. I nurtured hope that we hadn't ruined him after all. He was showing a strength of character that manifested itself in love and concern for others. Our Matt was going to make something of himself in spite of us.

My morning reverie was interrupted by the particularly sweet song of a robin. He seemed so happy as he perched on a limb high over my head, and my heart broke away from its review of my family to sing its own little song to accompany him.

Well, I thought when our song had ended, *the restlessness does not come because I do not appreciate the benefits that God has given me, nor does it come because I do not love my family.* Some of the feeling of guilt began to drain away from me. I felt much better having honestly discovered these facts.

So . . . I went on, *Why am I feeling restless? What is wrong with me?*

Nothing is wrong, the inner me replied. *As you said, you are not unappreciative nor uncaring. Yet it is true that you are restless. That does not prove that you are lacking, It is just time to move on, that's all.*

To move on? I was as incredulous as if the answer had come from a total stranger.

Certainly. What do you think brings the robin back each spring? It is not that he no longer has his nest nor his food supply. He just knows that it is time to move on.

But to move on WHERE? How?

You'll know when the time comes.

But I'm not sure that I want—

Hush.

I had never even considered "moving on" before. I was very much a "home person." I wasn't even especially taken with the idea of marriage. Oh, I supposed that somewhere, someday, there would be someone, but I certainly had no intention of going out looking for him, nor had I been very impressed with any of the young men who had come looking for me. On more than one occasion I had excused myself and happily turned them over to Julie. She also seemed pleased with the arrangement; but the feelings of the young men involved, I must shamefully confess, concerned me very little.

And now I was to "move on"?

The uneasiness within me changed to a new feeling—fear. Being a practical person and knowing full well that I wasn't prepared to deal with these new attitudes at the present, I pushed them out of my mind, entered the sedate brick school building and my third-grade classroom, and deliberately set myself to concentrating on the spelling exercise for the first class of the morning. Robert Ackley was still having problems. I had tried everything that I knew to help him. What could I possibly try next?

I went through the entire day with a seriousness and intent unfamiliar even to me. Never before had I put myself so totally into my lessons, to make them interesting and understandable. At the end of the day I was exhausted, so I decided to clean the blackboards and go home. Usually I spent an hour or so in preparation for the next day's lessons, but I just didn't feel up to it this time. I hurriedly dusted off the erasers, shoved some lesson books into my bag, securely fastened the classroom door behind me, and left the three-story building.

The walk home refreshed me somewhat; I even saw the robin with whom I had sung a duet that morning! I felt more like myself as I climbed our front steps and let myself in. Mother was in the small sunroom pouring tea that Martha, our maid, had brought. She didn't even seem surprised to see me home early.

"Lay aside your hat and join me," she called. I detected excitement in her voice.

I placed my light shawl and hat on the hall table and took a chair opposite Mother. I felt I could use a cup of strong, hot tea.

"I got a letter from Jonathan," Mother announced as she handed me my cup.

I assumed then that her excitement was due to Jonathan's letter, or the news that it contained.

Jonathan was still special to Mother. Being her firstborn and only child from her first marriage, he was also her first love in many ways. Julie had on occasion suggested that Mother loved Jonathan more than the rest of us. I tried to convince Julie that Mother did not love him *more*—just differently.

I often thought how difficult it must have been for her to give him up, to let him go. Jonathan had been just nineteen when he decided that he must go west. I was only four years old at the time and too young to really understand it all, but I had been aware after he left that something was different about our home, about Mother, though she tried hard not to let it affect the rest of us. Three months after Jonathan had left, baby Matthew had arrived, and Mother's world had taken on new meaning. Yet not even Matt had taken Jonathan's place in her heart.

And now Mother sat opposite me, calmly serving tea, though I could tell that she felt anything but calm. Whatever the news in Jonathan's letter, I sensed that Mother was excited rather than concerned, so her tenseness did not frighten me.

"How is he?" I asked, choosing to let Mother pick her own time and words for revealing her excitement.

"Oh, just fine. The family is well. Mary is feeling fine. She is due soon now. Jonathan's lumber business is growing. He had to hire another clerk last month."

It all sounded good. I was happy for this older brother whom I barely remembered, yet somehow I felt that Mother's present mood did not stem from any of the facts that she had so hurriedly stated. I mumbled a polite response about being glad for Jonathan's good fortune and sipped my tea. I did wish that Mother would get to the point.

Mother didn't even lift her cup; instead, she reached into the bosom of her gown and removed Jonathan's recent letter. We were all used to her doing that. Whenever a letter from Jonathan arrived, she would read it through a number of times and then tuck it in the front of her dress. She carried it around with her for days and would pull it forth and reread it whenever time allowed.

She carefully unfolded it now. But rather than pass it to me as she normally did, she began to hurriedly read aloud. She passed quickly through Jonathan's greetings as though she was anxious to get to the real heart of the letter. As I continued to sip my tea, I could hear the excitement growing in her voice. She suddenly slowed down, and I knew that she intended for me to hear and understand every word.

"'There is no end to opportunities here in the West. I know several men who came out with nothing and who now have great homes and flourishing businesses. All that one needs is determination, stamina, and a bit of horse sense.' "

Surely Mother isn't contemplating urging Papa to move West was the foolish thought that popped into my mind. Mother read on.

" 'I have given a great deal of thought to my family lately. It would be so good to have one of my own here. I miss you all so much. Especially you, Mother, but you know that.

" 'It's easy to think of the West as a man's land, and so it is; but there are plenty of opportunities here for women as well. And I might add that we in the West realize that if we are to grow strong, we need fine young women to make homes for our men and ensure proper families for our future.' "

I must have grimaced some as I thought, *What a cold, calculating way to look at marriage.* But Mother continued without interruption—I had missed a few words.

" '. . . so I thought of Elizabeth.' "

Confusing thoughts exploded in my mind. *Elizabeth? Me? Me WHAT? Is he suggesting that I go bargain-hunting for some western shopkeeper or backwoods rancher for a husband? Not me! Never! Never!* I felt that I would rather die first.

The blood had drained from my face as I started to rise from my chair. "Never," I whispered to myself. But Mother had paid no attention to my soft gasp and hurried on.

" 'Teachers are sorely needed here. Many mothers in country areas still must tutor their children. But these women have little time and no training. We are anxious to change all of that. We want our next generations to be well educated, because in the future we hope to pick the leaders of our new province from among our own.

" 'You say that Elizabeth is a fine teacher and a sensible young woman—and I am sure that she is. I talked today with a school superintendent whom I know. He is short of teachers, and some of those that he does have, he would replace if he could. He says that if Elizabeth is willing to come west, he would gratefully give her a position, and, as I said before, it would be so good to have someone from my family here.' "

Stunned, I watched Mother's eyes continue on down the page, but she was reading silently now. I got the impression that I was temporarily forgotten and that her thoughts were with her beloved son Jonathan somewhere out West.

I was glad for those few moments to compose myself before I had to meet her eyes again. Jonathan was actually proposing that I go west. For what? Before he had suggested the teaching opportunities, he had written that they needed young women to "ensure proper families." Well, I in no way intended to help them do that. Definitely not!

I hoped that Mother wouldn't be too hard on Jonathan when she replied to the letter. I knew that he had meant well, though he must have known that our mother would never agree to a daughter of hers, on the pretense of teaching, going off to the wilds to find herself a man. *Even if that isn't Jonathan's intent at all,* I reasoned, *and he is simply looking for more teachers, I have a perfectly good teaching position right where I am.*

Mother finished reading Jonathan's rather lengthy letter and again tucked it in her bosom. Her tea had grown cold, but she absently reached for her cup and sipped from it with a far-away look in her eyes. I was on the verge of, "Look, Mother, don't let it upset you. Jonathan meant well, but you needn't fear. I have no intention of taking it seriously, . . ." when she lifted her eyes from her cup and looked directly at me. I expected a mild reprimand of Jonathan, but instead she said simply, "Well?" She smiled at me, and I could easily detect eagerness in her voice.

I was startled and flustered.

"Well?" I questioned back, wondering just what she meant. I couldn't understand Mother's rather extraordinary reaction to Jonathan's preposterous proposal. *Is she actually thinking that I would even give the matter consideration? How CAN she? Surely she must see that it is totally . . .* And then in a flash it came to me. I was to be Mother's love-offering to Jonathan, his "piece-of-the-family" presented to him over the miles. Somehow my going west to be with him would bring comfort to my mother's heart.

I loved her. She was a dear mother. Never would I wish to hurt her. I didn't dare bluntly blurt out that the whole idea was outlandish and that Jonathan had been foolish even to suggest it. With Mother sitting there before me, the "well" still lingering in her gaze, I couldn't say no. But could I say yes? Definitely not. But I could say maybe, until I had taken time to think this whole thing through, to sort it out in my mind, and to plan some way I could get out of it without hurting my mother.

"Well—it's—it's such a surprise. I'd—I'd never thought of the possibility of leaving—of going . . ."

My mind fumbled about for words but found none to still the look of concern creeping into Mother's eyes. I willed my confused mind into control and hurried on.

"It sounds—interesting—very interesting." I tried to put some sparkle into my voice, but it was difficult when I could hardly get the words past my tight throat.

Mother relaxed some, and her eyes began to shine again. It was a moment before I realized that they were bright with unshed tears. I felt almost panicky. I *couldn't* disappoint her—at least not at the moment. I tried to swallow away the lump in my throat and forced a smile as I put down the fragile china cup.

"It's—well—I'll—I'll do some thinking about it and we'll—well, we'll see. . . ."

Mother reached out and touched my hand. The tears spilled a bit from her eyes, wetting her dark lashes and dropping onto her cheeks.

"Beth," she said, "there is no one whom I would rather send to Jonathan than you."

I was touched, but frightened. I swallowed hard again, attempted another smile, and rose from my chair. After a light kiss on Mother's forehead, I excused myself. I had to get away, alone, where I could think. My whole world was spinning around, and I felt that if I didn't soon get control of things, I would end up hurling off somewhere into space.

I was willing to *consider* being Jonathan's love-package-from-home, for Mother's sake. Yes, I was even willing to consider teaching out West. But as for marrying some uncouth, unkempt man out of the frontier, *there* I drew a definite, solid line. Never!

Later that evening, Papa knocked quietly at my door. I had been trying to read in bed, a luxury that I normally enjoyed, but somehow Jane Austen's young women had failed to intrigue me.

He walked to my window and stood looking out at the quietness of the city. The street lamps flickered softly against the gathering darkness. I waited for him to speak; but when he said nothing, I laid aside my book, pushed myself up to a sitting position, and asked softly, "You've talked to Mother?"

He cleared his throat and turned from the window. He still didn't speak—just nodded his head.

"And what do you think?" I asked, secretly hoping that he would exclaim that the whole idea was outrageous and unthinkable. He didn't.

"Well—," he said, pulling up a chair beside my bed, "at first it was a bit of a shock. But after I thought it through for a while, I began to understand why your mother is rather excited about the whole thing. I guess it could be an adventure for you, Elizabeth, and, it would seem, not too risky a one."

"Then you think I should—"

"Consider it? Yes, consider it. Go? Not necessarily. Only you will be able to decide that. You know that you are loved and wanted here, but should you want this—this new experience, we will not hold you back."

"I don't know, Papa. It's all so—so new. I don't know what to think about it."

"Elizabeth, we trust you to make the right decision, *for you.* Your mother and I have agreed to abide by it. Whatever you decide, we want it to be what *you* feel you should do. Your mother, as much as she would love to see you go to Jonathan, does not want you to feel pressured to do so if it's not what you want. She asked me to tell you that, Elizabeth. She is afraid that your loyalty and desire to please her might lead you to go for her sake. That's not enough reason to make such a life-changing decision, Elizabeth."

"Oh, Papa! Right now I'm all butterflies. I never dreamed—"

"Don't hurry, my dear. Such a decision needs much careful thinking and praying. Your mother and I will be standing behind you."

"Thank you, Papa."

He kissed my forehead and squeezed my hand.

"Whatever you decide . . ." he whispered as he left my room.

I didn't pick up Jane Austen's book again. I knew that now for certain I couldn't concentrate on the words. So I pulled the chain to put out the lamp and punched my pillows into what I hoped would be a sleep-inducing position. With the covers tucked carefully about me, I settled down for the night. It didn't work. It was a long time until I was able to fall asleep.

TWO

The First Step

The next few days were full of soul searching. I was so preoccupied that I sometimes wondered if I were actually teaching my students. They didn't seem to notice any difference in me, so I guess that I was at least going through the proper motions.

As she promised, Mother didn't press me; but I could sense that she was anxiously waiting for my decision. I knew that she was praying too. I did hope that she truly was leaving it to the Father's will and not merely pleading for Him to "send me forth."

I wavered—which was unusual for me. One moment I would think of all those that I loved: my family, my students, my church friends; and I would inwardly cry out, "I can't go, I just can't!" The next instant I would think of that part of my family in the West. Something invisible was drawing me to the older brother whom I had never really known. I also thought of all those children without a teacher, and I knew that they, too, wished to learn. I even considered the great adventure that this new opportunity held, and I would find myself reasoning, *Why not? Maybe this is the answer to the restlessness within me. Maybe I should go. . . .*

Back and forth my feelings swung, like the pendulum on our grandfather clock.

After considerable debate and prayer and thought, I felt directed to Joshua 1:9: "Be strong and of a good courage; be not afraid, neither be thou dismayed: for the Lord thy God is with thee whithersoever thou goest."

I repeated the passage out loud and felt my anxieties relax into peace. I would go.

Mother was almost beside herself with joy and excitement when

I told her. Julie begged to go with me. I loved Julie and I was sure that there would be many times in the future when I would wish for her company; but the thought of trying to watch over a girl like Julie, in a land filled with men looking for brides, fairly made me shiver. I was glad when Papa and Mother promptly told her no.

Another month, and the school year came to a close. I waved good-bye to the last pupil, packed up all my books and teaching aids, and closed the door of the classroom carefully behind me for the last time. Blinking back some tears, I said good-bye to my fellow teachers and walked away from the school without looking back.

I had let Mother tell Jonathan about my decision, and he seemed overjoyed that I actually was coming. He even wrote a letter to *me,* telling me so directly. His and Mother's excitement seemed to be contagious, and my desire to see my brother was growing daily.

Jonathan had passed the word to the school superintendent, and he, too, hurried a letter off to me. Mr. Higgins (the name somehow suited my mental image of him) assured me that he was pleased to hear that I would be coming west; and, his letter stated, he would give care and consideration in assigning me to the school that he felt was right for me, and he would be most anxious to meet me upon my arrival.

The days, filled with shopping, packing, and finally shipping my belongings, passed quickly.

Jonathan had said that anything I could spare should be shipped early. The freight cars had a tendency to get shuttled aside at times and often took longer for the trip than the passenger cars. I secretly wondered if Jonathan wasn't using this as a ploy, reasoning that the shipped-ahead trunks would be a measure of insurance against a girl who at the last moment might wish to change her mind.

It could have happened, too. When the day arrived that Papa and I took my trunks to the freight station and I presented my belongings to the man behind the counter, the realization fully hit me that I was taking a giant step into the unknown. Somewhat dazed, I watched my trunks being weighed and ticketed and finally carted away from the checking desk on a hand-pulled wagon. In those trunks were my books, bedding, personal effects, and almost my entire wardrobe. It seemed to me that a large part of my life was being routinely trundled away. For a moment fear again tightened my throat, and I had an impulse to dash out and gather those trunks back to myself and hurry back to the familiar comfort of my own home and room. Instead, I turned quickly and almost stumbled out of the building. Papa had to break into full stride in order to catch up to me.

"Well, that's cared for," I said in a whispery voice, trying to intimate that I was glad to scratch one more task from my awesome list. I think that Papa saw through my bluff, He answered me heartily but completely off the subject. "Saw a delightful little hat in that smart little shop beside Eatons. I thought at the time it was just made for you. Shall we go and take a look at it?"

Some men despise being seen in a lady's shop. My father was not one of them. Perhaps it had something to do with the fact that he had four daughters and an attractive wife. Papa loved to see his women dressed prettily and took pleasure in helping us to choose nice things. Besides, he was well aware of the fact that a new hat was often good medicine for feminine woes—especially when the difficulty was no more serious than a butterfly stomach.

I smiled at him, appreciative of his sensitivity. Who would pamper me when I was away from Papa? I took his arm and together we headed for the little shop.

Papa was right. The hat did suit me well; the emerald-green velvet looked just right with my dark gold hair and hazel eyes. I liked it immediately and was glad that he had spotted it. In fact, I decided right then and there that I would wear it upon my arrival in Calgary. It would give me a measure of confidence, and I had a feeling I would need all of it that I could get.

As we rumbled home in our motor car, I again thought of what a thoughtful man I had for a father. I reached over and placed my hand on the arm of his well-cut suit. I would miss him. I used my handkerchief to wipe some tears from my eyes, murmuring something about the wind in my face. There was still a week before I would board the train. I didn't need to get soft and sentimental yet.

THREE
On the Way

I fidgeted on the worn leather of the train seat, willing my nerves to quit jumping and my heart to quit its thunderous beating. I would soon be arriving in Calgary. The very name with its unfamiliar ring made my pulse race.

I would soon be seeing my brother Jonathan. My memories were vaguely outlined in the shadowy figure of a tall, gangly youth with a strong will of his own. I would also be meeting his wife, Mary, whom he declared to be the sweetest and most beautiful woman on the face of the earth. And I would be introduced to four little children—one nephew and three nieces. I was prepared for them, having purchased sweets at our last stop. Children were easy to win, but would my brother and my sister-in-law be pleased with me? Was I ready to step out of the relative safety of the train into a strange, new world?

My four slow-moving days on the Pacific Western, spent sitting stiffly in cramped train seats, and even slower-passing nights, had been gradually preparing me. I finally had been able to overcome my intense homesickness. The first three days I had missed my family to such an extent that I feared I might become ill. Gradually the ache had left, and in its place there now seemed to be only a hollow.

As the pain had left me, I had been able to find some interest in the landscape, which seemed amazingly different from what I was accustomed. Jonathan had tried to describe the land to me in his letters, but I had not visualized the emptiness, the barrenness, the vastness of it all. As I gazed out the train window, it seemed that we traveled on forever, seeing hardly any people. Occasionally we did pass small herds of animals—antelope, deer and even a few buffalo, roving slowly across the prairie, and delaying the train once in a while as they lazily crossed the iron tracks.

I had expected to see Indian teepees scattered all across the countryside. But in fact, I saw very few Indians at all, and they were almost all in the small towns that we passed through, looking very "civilized" indeed. I saw no braves painted for the warpath. Most Indian people moved quietly along the streets, concerned only with their own trading activities.

Now we were nearing the frontier town of Calgary, the home of my brother Jonathan and many other adventuresome persons. What would it be like? Would it be at all modern? After I had made my decision to go, Julie had read all she could find about the West. Where she discovered all of her information, I never did learn; but at any hour of the day or night that she could corner me, she would announce new "facts" she had gathered. According to her, the West was full of reckless, daring men, so eager for a wife that they often stole one. (I wasn't sure that she disapproved.) Julie painted word pictures of cowboys, voyageurs, miners, and lumbermen—all roaming the dusty streets in their travel-stained leather and fur, looking for excitement, women, wealth, and danger, though not necessarily in that order. And Indians—everywhere Indians. Though most were rather peaceable now, she was sure they still wouldn't hesitate to take a scalp if the opportunity existed. This irrepressible sister of mine had even dared to whisper that perhaps I should bob my hair so none of them would be overly tempted by my heavy mass of waves. She warned me that they might find my dark gold curls with their red highlights irresistible.

"My scalp, complete with its hair, is quite safe from the Indians," I had assured Julie, but I will admit that she made me shiver a few times. She had nodded solemnly and informed me that I was probably right and it was all due to the fortunate fact that the West now had the North West Mounted Police. According to Julie, they were the West's knights in red-serge armor, and Calgary abounded with them. Should the need ever arise, a lady had only to call, and Red Coats would come running. Judging from the sparkle in Julie's eye as she described this scene, I would have expected her to avail herself of their services quite regularly.

Julie had also claimed that Calgary was a land of perpetual blizzard. It stopped snowing only long enough to allow an occasional "chinook" to blow through, and then the cold and neck-deep snow would again take over.

Calgary was now only minutes away, according to the conductor, and on this August afternoon, with the hot sun beating down unmercifully upon the stuffy coach, I realized that Julie had been wrong at least on this one point—unless, of course, this was just one of those chinooks. Still, I couldn't help but wonder if Julie may have been mistaken about some other "facts" as well. I would soon see. In my impatience I stood up to pace the floor.

There really wasn't much room for walking, and I got the impression that my stalking back and forth in the narrow aisle was irritating to some of the other passengers. I smiled my sweetest smile at those nearest to me. "After sitting so long, I simply must work some of the knots out of my muscles before we reach Calgary," I explained. I hoped that they didn't realize it was in reality nerves rather than stiffness that drove me from my seat.

I walked to the end of the aisle and was nearly hit by the door when it swung open before the returning conductor. He looked at me with a startled expression and then got on with his job which was at this point to call out in a booming voice, "Calgary!—Calgary!" He passed through the car and into the next, still calling.

A bustle of activity followed in his wake as people gathered their belongings, said good-byes to new acquaintances, donned jackets or shawls, and put on bonnets or hats that had been laid aside. I used the reflection from the window glass to adjust my new green bonnet.

The train blew a long, low whistle. One could almost feel exhausted thinking of the amount of steam necessary to produce such a sound. Then the clickity-clack of the wheels began to slow down till I was sure that if one would choose to concentrate on the task, each revolution could be counted. We were now traveling past some buildings. They appeared rather new and were scattered some distance apart. Most were constructed of wood rather than the brick or masonry which I was used to back home. A few of the newest ones were made of sandstone. The streets were not cobblestoned, but dusty and busy. Men and, thankfully, some women too, hurried back and forth with great purpose. The train jerked to a stop with a big hiss from within its iron innards like a giant sigh that the long journey was finally over. I sighed too as I stood and gathered my things from the seat where I had piled them neatly together. Working my way toward the door, half-step by half-step in the slow-moving line of fellow passengers, I couldn't keep my eyes from the windows. It was all so new, so different. I was relieved to spot many men in business suits among the waiting crowd. It was a comfort of sorts to realize that the men of the West were not all rough-and-ready adventurers.

And then through the crowd, seeming head and shoulders above all others, I noticed two men in red tunics and broad-brimmed Stetsons. Julie's Mounties! I smiled to myself at the thought of her excitement if she were here! Even their walk seemed to denote purposefulness, and though people nodded greetings to them, the crowd seemed to automatically part before them out of respect. I bent down a bit so that I could get a better view of them through the window. I was immediately bumped from behind by a package tucked beneath the arm of a rough-looking man with a cigar in his mouth. I flushed and straightened quickly, not daring to meet his eyes.

When it was finally my turn, I carefully stepped down, grateful for the assistance of the conductor with all my parcels and a small suitcase. When I had negotiated the steps, I looked up into the smiling eyes of an almost stranger—yet somehow I knew instantly that it was Jonathan. Without a moment's hesitation I dropped what I was carrying and threw my arms around his neck.

FOUR

Calgary

Despite my proper upbringing, I was sorely tempted to stare at everything that our automobile passed on the way to Jonathan's house. Never in my life had I seen a town like Calgary! Cowboys on horseback maneuvered expertly between automobiles and pedestrians in the dusty street. Two ladies, their long skirts lifted daintily, crossed quickly in front of us. And there was a real Indian, in dark coat and formal hat with a long braid down his back! I tried desperately not to let my extreme fascination at the interesting activities around me show, but I guess I failed.

Jonathan chuckled, "Calgary is a show-off, isn't it, Elizabeth?" As the color moved slowly into my cheeks, he courteously turned his eyes back to the road so as not to embarrass me further. He had not lived so long in the West as to forget that it was improper for a lady to stare.

"Do you know that I've lived in this town for almost sixteen years, and I still can't believe what is happening here?" Jonathan continued matter-of-factly. "It seems that every time I drive through the streets another building has sprung up. It reminds me of when I was a child at Christmastime. I went to bed at night with the familiar parlor as usual; but in the morning, there was a bedecked tree, festooned with all manner of strings and baubles and glittering candles. The magic of it! No wonder children can easily accept fantasy. And this is almost like a fantasy, don't you think, Elizabeth?"

I could only nod my agreement, too spellbound to speak. I turned my head to glance back over the way that we had just come. We had climbed steadily as we left downtown Calgary. Jonathan's home must be up on a hill rather than in the valley beside the river.

As I looked back down the street, I could see the buildings of Calgary stretched out across the flatness of the valley. Water sparkled in many places, reflecting the afternoon sun. I looked in awe at the scene and finally found my voice.

"The river—it seems to twist and turn all around. Everywhere I look, there seems to be another part of the stream."

Jonathan laughed. "There are *two* rivers that merge down there. They're called the Bow and the Elbow."

"Unusual names."

"Yes, I guess they are. You'll find a number of strange names in the West."

I smiled. "Well," I conceded, "I will admit that we have our share of strange names in the East, too."

Jonathan nodded, a grin spreading over his face, and I could almost see names like Trois-Rivieres and Cap-de-la-Madelaine flitting across his mind.

"Tell me about Calgary." I just couldn't wait to learn something about this intriguing town.

Jonathan gave me an understanding smile.

"Where do I start?" he asked himself. "Calgary was founded as a fort for the North West Mounted Police in 1875—not so long ago, really. It was first named Fort Brisebois, but Macleod, the commander, didn't care much for that name, I guess. He renamed her Fort Calgary—this is a Gaelic word, meaning clear, running water—after his birthplace in Scotland."

"Clear, running water," I repeated. "I like it. It suits it well."

I looked again at the portions of the rivers that gleamed between the buildings and the thick tree growth of the valley.

Jonathan continued, "After the railroad was built in 1883, people began to take seriously the settling of the West. It was much easier to load one's belongings on a train than it had been to venture overland by wagon. And with the train, the women were even able to bring with them some of the finer things of life that previously had to remain behind.

"In the earlier days mostly adventurers or opportunists moved westward, and though a fair share of those still came, many dedicated men and women arrived each year hoping to make a home for themselves in this new land."

"It was still difficult, wasn't it?" I questioned.

"Fortunately for us, the Mounties got here before the bulk of the settlers. The new people at least had law to appeal to if the need arose—and the need often did. The Indians had already learned that the Red Coat could be trusted—that a law-breaker, no matter the color of his skin, would be brought to justice. The Mounties helped to make Calgary, and the area around it, a safe place for women and children."

"That doesn't sound like the West which Julie told me about."

"Oh, we've had our skirmishes, to be sure, but they've been few and far between; and the North West Mounted Police have been able to restore control rather quickly."

"Have the Indians been *that* bothersome?" I asked, wondering if Julie had been right after all.

"Indians? Can't rightly blame the Indians. Most of the trouble comes from the makers of fire-water."

"Fire-water?"

"Whiskey. Well, I guess it can't really be called whiskey, either. It was known more often as—pardon me, please—as 'rot-gut.' It had an alcohol base, but the brewers threw in about everything they could find to give it taste and color—pepper, chewing tobacco, almost anything. Don't know how anyone could drink the stuff, but some braves sold furs, their ponies—even at times a squaw—just to get hold of a few bottles."

"That's terrible!"

"It ruined many of the choicest young Indian men. Threatened whole tribes, at times. Some of the chiefs saw the danger and hated the rotten stuff, but they were hard put to control its evil. Wicked, horrible stuff! A real disgrace to the white men who peddled it at the expense of wasted, human lives." Jonathan shook his head, and

I could tell that the previous trade of illegal liquor disturbed him greatly.

"Anyway," he continued, brightening, "the North West Mounted Police were organized, found their way west in spite of extreme hardship, and went right to work on the problem. Their first big job was to clean up Fort Whoop-Up."

"Whoop-Up," I chuckled. "That's even stranger than Elbow. Is that around here?"

"Doesn't even exist anymore. It was in Southern Alberta about six miles from where Lethbridge is now located. They say the things that went on there would make your hair curl. Old Johnny Healy operated the place, and his vile concoction could purchase about anything he wanted. One cup of his whiskey would buy him a choice buffalo robe. Old Johnny made himself rich. He gathered together a group of rascals with like leanings—rum-runners, wolvers, law-dodgers, and the like. He built himself a nice little fort for them all to flock together in. Nobody knows exactly how many were living there; in fact, the estimates seem to vary a lot, but, at any rate, it seems that there were *too* many. At times they went too far, drank their own whiskey and went on the rampage. It was some of the wolvers who eventually brought the whole thing to an end. They were led by a man who had, somewhere in his past, developed a real hatred for the Indians. He had already shown his hostility on more than one occasion. When a few bucks made off with his ponies, it wasn't enough for him to try to get his horses back. Instead, he used it as an excuse to start shooting. He and his men murdered several Indians at a place called Cypress Hills—they didn't seem to care that those Indians weren't even of the same tribe as the horse thieves."

"Was nothing done?"

"Word got back East, along with an urgent appeal to Prime Minister Sir John A. McDonald. He sped up the organization of the new police force for the West and sent them out as quickly as possible. That's why the North West Mounted Police were hurried westward."

"To bring justice, law and order to the West?"

"Right! From the start they had their work cut out for them. One of their jobs was to gain the confidence and respect of the Indians. After what had been happening between the Indians and the whites, you can believe that job wasn't any small task. But they managed it. The white offenders were brought to trial, and the Indians began to see that they had friends in the Force who wore red coats.

"The motto of the new Force was 'Maintien le Droit'—'Uphold the Right,' and they worked hard and long to accomplish just that."

"And the Indians did learn to accept them?" I asked.

"I guess Red Crow, the head chief of the Blackfoot Nation, sort of summed it up when he signed the treaty of 1877. This wise and cunning old man was speaking of Macleod at the time, but the same could have been said about the other commanders of the Force as well. Red Crow said, 'He has made many promises, and *kept* them all.' "

I had sat motionless, listening to Jonathan. What if Julie had been there to hear him? Thanks to all of the romantic notions with which she had filled her mind, she would be swooning at the very possibility of meeting one of the West's great heroes in red! Even with my more practical outlook, I was stirred by this background on the Mounties and their part in Canadian history. Certainly many men and women—not to mention a nation—owed them a great debt of gratitude. I added my thanks to the already lengthy list, then promptly shifted my thoughts to the present, content to place the North West Mounted Police back in history where I felt they belonged.

"How much farther?" I asked Jonathan.

"I must confess," he answered with a twinkle in his eye, "I have taken you on the scenic route. We could have been home several minutes ago, but I just couldn't wait to show you our—" He stopped in mid-sentence and looked at me with concern. "You must be tired, Elizabeth. I'm afraid my enthusiasm was ill-timed."

"Oh, no. I'm fine. I've truly enjoyed it," I quickly assured him.

"It's all so new and so different, I'm—"

"Just one more thing, and I'll hurry you home—Mary will have my hide anyway. She's so anxious to meet you, and so are the children."

We topped a hill, and there before us was the most beautiful scene that I had ever beheld. I had seen glimpses of the mountains as the train rolled toward Calgary, but the panorama which lay before me now was indescribable. The mountains seemed near enough to smell the tang of the crisp air and feel the freshness of the winds. I didn't say anything. I couldn't. I sat and looked and loved every minute of it. Jonathan was pleased. He loved the mountains; I could sense that.

"That," he said at length, "is why I would never want to leave the West."

"It's beautiful beyond description," I finally managed to say, exhilaration springing up within like a fountain. To live and move and work in the shadow of those awe-inspiring mountains was more than I had ever dreamed of. A little prayer welled up within me, *Thank you, God, for the unexpected. Thank you for pushing me out of my secure nest.*

All too soon, it seemed, Jonathan turned the automobile around, and headed us down the hill and back into town.

FIVE

Family

Mary was waiting at the door when we pulled up in front of the house and she ran to meet me as I stepped down from the auto. She pulled me into a warm embrace almost before my feet had a chance to properly settle on the ground. I was glad for the enthusiastic welcome and immediately felt I was with family.

I studied the woman who was Jonathan's wife, my sister-in-law. A wealth of reddish-brown hair was scooped rather casually in a pinned-up style. Curly wisps of it teased about her face and neck, giving her a girlish look. Her green eyes sparked with merriment and her full mouth produced the warmest of smiles. I smiled in return.

"Oh, Elizabeth," she exclaimed, "it is so good to meet you!"

"And you, Mary," I returned. "You are just as Jonathan described you."

She hurried me toward the house to meet the children while Jonathan busied himself in gathering up my belongings.

We passed right through the main hall and out a back door to a shaded yard that seemed to be filled with shouting, wiggling small bodies. These were my nieces and nephew. At once they made a dash for me; they were not at all reserved or inhibited. It did appear that they believed the coming of an aunt was a great event.

When Mary had restored order, I was able to meet each one of them in a quieter fashion.

At eight, William, the eldest, looked like Jonathan except that his hair had a reddish tinge which he had inherited from Mary. Sarah, six, was small and dainty; if any of the offspring could have been deemed retiring, Sarah would have been the one. Kathleen was next. This four-year-old looked like she should have been a boy; mischief sparkled out of her intensely blue eyes, and her pixie face was always fixed in a grin. Baby Elizabeth, named for my mother, had only recently joined the family and was much too young to take part in the present merry-making. She slept through the whole commotion.

After a quick tour of the house, the evening meal was served, and we gathered around the table. Jonathan believed that the family should share this special time of day, and so the children joined us at the table. As I watched them clamber into chairs, I wondered just what Mother would have thought of the whole event. In our home, children, even quiet, well-mannered ones, did not join the adults at the table until they had passed their twelfth, or at the earliest, tenth birthday.

Jonathan's children proved to be well-behaved in spite of their high spirits, and we adults were able to converse, uninterrupted by childish outbursts. It was obvious that they had been instructed well as to how to conduct themselves. *Maybe it is wise to start them young at the family dinner table,* I decided as I watched them. I did wonder as I studied Kathleen just how long she would be able to sit primly like a little lady. She looked like a miniature volcano about to erupt.

The meal, served by a maid named Stacy, was absolutely delicious. I was embarrassed at the amount of food I ate. Jonathan assured me that the crisp air affected one's appetite; I was glad to have something to blame it on.

"I'm so glad that you could come a few days early," Mary said. "Now we have opportunity to get to know you before you commence your teaching duties. We do want to show you around, and—" she added with a twinkle in her eye, "to show you off."

I smiled at her.

"Indeed," teased Jonathan, "I have a whole list of young men waiting to meet you. I finally gave up trying to keep track of who was to be first. I told them that they would just have to stand in line and wait their turn, but I'm afraid . . ."

My cheeks grew warm and I interrupted Jonathan before he

could go on. "I'm quite happy to meet your friends," I announced firmly, "but I do want to make one thing clear: I came west to *teach,* not to *wed.* Had I been interested in matrimony, I could have stayed in the East and found an acceptable spouse. Julie, who by the way is our family expert on the subject, assures me that the men of the West are adventurers—undependable, rough, and rowdy. I don't know if her research is totally reliable, but I've no intention of finding out. If you want a wife for one of your friends, you'd best bring out Julie. She'll be more than willing to consider the possibility. I? Never!"

It was a rather long speech under the circumstances, and the faces of the listeners changed from unbelief, to concern, to amusement. When I finished, I saw Jonathan steal a glance at Mary to see if she considered me serious. She gave him a barely visible nod, and he understood her to mean that I was. He cleared his throat, then waited a moment.

"I see," he said slowly, "that we shouldn't tease you so. Here we often forget the manners that our mothers tried so hard to instill in us. We tease and jest all the time. It helps the road to smooth out when it might otherwise be rough.

"Of course we have no intention of marrying you off." He then added with great sincerity, "But I could this night, personally, introduce you to a dozen good, clean, mannerly, well-bred gentlemen who would make your Eastern dandies look pale in comparison. But I won't do it," he hurried on, "lest my intentions be misconstrued."

I knew exactly what he was implying and realized with embarrassment that I deserved this mild rebuke for my tactlessness and bad manners. My face was suddenly drained of all color. I knew that I should apologize for my outburst, but somehow I couldn't get the words through my tight throat.

Jonathan chuckled, and the sound of his soft laugh eased the tension around the table. "I promise, little sister," he said with feigned seriousness, "to make no effort to see you married if you have no desire to be so. But, looking at you, I'd say you will have to get that message across yourself to more than one young man."

Mary seemed to agree. She didn't say anything—only smiled—but the warmth of that smile carried with it approval of her sister-in-law's appearance.

My cheeks flushed again, for a different reason this time. I was willing to assume the responsibility of getting that message across, if need be.

"I've had to do it before," I said calmly, "and I'm quite confident that I can again."

A small voice broke in. "When I grow up, I'm gonna marry Dee."

Everyone shared in the laughter; even I, who did not have the slightest notion who Dee was.

As Mary wiped the tears of laughter from her eyes she attempted to enlighten me. "Dee is a very dear friend. He's already close to thirty and as determined as you, my dear, to stay single."

"He's *my* friend," Kathleen insisted.

"Of course he is, sweetie. Now finish your dinner."

When we rose from the table, a wave of tiredness flooded over me. I wondered if I'd be able to hold out while Mary went to tuck in the children.

It was early yet, and I knew that it was unthinkable to ask to be shown to my room, and yet that was the very thing that I longed to do. Jonathan noticed it.

"You must be dead on your feet. Why don't you go and have a warm bath and get to bed early tonight? I never could get a proper night's sleep on one of those rumbling trains. The time change makes a difference too. According to Eastern time, it's now your bedtime."

I admitted that I was terribly weary.

"Go on, then," he insisted. "Your door is the first one on the right at the top of the stairs. The bath is in the room next to yours. After your long trip I'm sure you will enjoy relaxing in a tub again. I've already put your things in your room. I'm off to hear the children's prayers now, so I'll tell Mary. She will understand. There's plenty of time ahead for us to catch up on everything."

I thanked him and climbed the stairs. I could hardly wait to crawl into that tub. I sincerely hoped I would still have the energy to make it from the tub to the bed.

Soon I would need to write Mother and tell her all about Jonathan's lovely home and beautiful family. It was evident that the West had dealt very kindly with him. Mother would be proud. Jonathan himself had been very modest in his letters home, but I had no inhibitions about painting for Mother the complete picture.

Jonathan's home, a large three-story dwelling with many gables and bay windows, was a lovely structure of red brick; the elaborate wooden trim around the whole house was painted white.

The interior was spacious and cool, furnished with pieces shipped from the East. Colorful carpets covered the floors, and rich draperies softened the windows. Only Jonathan's study showed the unique influence of the West. Here was locally built furniture, massive and impressive. The wall bore mounted animal heads. A bear rug sprawled in front of the fireplace, while a buffalo robe covered the couch.

But the letter would have to wait. Tonight I was too tired to even consider writing. Tonight I wanted only a bed. Tomorrow—well, tomorrow I hoped to somehow have another look at those gorgeous mountains. I would attempt to tell my family back East about them as well, but already I knew that whatever I could say would never do the mountains justice.

SIX

Introductions

It did appear indeed that Jonathan and Mary were anxious to show me around, and to show me off. Never had I spent such a busy ten days as those that followed my arrival in Calgary. It seemed as though I was constantly changing my dress for the next occasion. But I will admit that it was all exciting, and I'm afraid it threatened to go to my head.

I had arrived on a Friday and Jon (I discovered that he favored being called Jon, so I complied, though it did seem a shame to go from a beautiful name like Jonathan to one as simple as Jon)—anyway, Jon and Mary decided that after my long train journey, I needed Saturday to rest. I didn't rest much, for I needed to unpack my clothes for my stay. I spent most of the day washing and pressing my things.

I was able to get to know my nephew and nieces, for everywhere I went, there they were at my elbow. It was delightful.

William had already finished two years in the classroom and was held in awe by his sisters. Sarah would shyly plead, "Show me, William—tell me—'splain it to me, William." William did, his self-esteem showing in those hazel eyes under his shock of reddish hair.

Kathleen was a dear. Her expressions sparkled with mischief as she chattered and watched everything that I did. It was apparent that Jon and Mary were parents who carefully guided and controlled their children, for even the energetic and outgoing Kathleen was not bold in her venturing, though her eyes showed that she found it difficult to restrain her bursts of enthusiasm.

As I unfolded an emerald-green velvet frock from the tissues that I had carefully wrapped it in, her eyes took on a special shine, and one hand reached out to touch the softness of the velvet. She quickly checked herself and tucked both hands behind her back where they would be safe from temptation. Her eyes sought mine, their message a plea for forgiveness for what she had almost done; but soon they were filled with a gentle question.

"Does it feel like baby chickies?" she asked in almost a whisper.

"You know," I answered honestly, "I have never, ever had the privilege of touching a baby chickie."

"You haven't?" Her eyes were big, and I knew that she could scarcely believe my ill fortune. A look of sympathy followed the wonder.

"I'll tell Papa," she said, very matter-of-factly, and I knew that she was confident Papa would care for my obvious need.

"Have you held baby chicks?" I asked her.

"Oh, yes."

"Then you touch the dress and tell me if it feels the same."

She looked at me, her big eyes wondering if I really meant it. I moved the dress nearer to her to assure her that I did. She slowly reached out one hand and then stopped herself, her eyes meeting mine with a twinkle as she said, "Oh—Oh." The hands were both turned palms up. "I'd better wash them first."

"They look fine to me."

She shrugged. "I'd better wash them anyway. Mama says some dirt don't see—don't look—" She struggled for the right word.

"Doesn't show?"

"Yah."

She ran hastily from the room and was soon back. She had splashed water on her dress in her hurry, and the hands that she had been so concerned about were still damp where the towel had not been given a chance to do its proper job. She finished drying them by wiping them up and down on the sides of her dress as she approached the velvet gown. She stood for a moment looking at its richness. Then she reached out slowly and touched a fold. Gently the little hand stroked the cloth, careful to brush it only in one direction.

"It does," she whispered, "and like a new kitten, too."

I reached down and pulled her to me.

"Baby chicks must feel nice; and I *have* stroked a new kitten, so I know *that* feels nice—but do you know what feels the nicest of all?"

She tipped back her head and studied my face.

"Little people," I said softly.

"Like boys and—and girls?"

"Boys and girls."

She giggled, and then threw her arms around my neck and hugged me. I swallowed hard. How wonderful to be able to hold a child, to love unreservedly and have the love returned.

Sarah called, and Kathleen released her hold.

"She's probl'y gonna say, 'Kathleen, wash for lunch,' and I've already washed!" She took great pleasure in the fact that she would be able to side-step the command. She started a lopsided skip as she left the room, not yet old enough to do it properly. At the door she stopped and turned back. "Thank you, Aunt Beth," she called. She threw me a kiss, which I returned, and was gone.

A few minutes later we were indeed gathered for lunch. William held us up because he was off climbing trees with a neighbor; it took Sarah several minutes to locate him. He was scolded gently and sent to wash and change his shirt, which had a ragged tear on one sleeve. He reappeared a few minutes later, fresh shirt properly buttoned but not so properly tucked in, and his face and hands scrubbed, though one could easily see the water line at his chin. Mary's rueful smile accepted him as he was, and the meal was served.

"After lunch I want you children to play outside—*in the yard,*" said Mary, looking pointedly at William. "Aunt Beth may want to nap."

"Oh, no," I hurried to explain, "I still haven't finished caring for my clothes."

Even as I said the words I realized just how much I would love to take time for a little rest.

"Baby Lis'beth still naps," Kathleen said seriously, and I could tell that she felt very proud about being allowed to go without an afternoon sleep.

"Baby Elizabeth is lucky," declared Mary. I guessed that there were many days when she gladly would have curled up for a nap herself if she had been given the opportunity.

Kathleen did not argue, though it was evident from the look in her eyes that she did not agree with her mother.

The next morning, Sunday, the house was filled with activity as we prepared to attend the church service. Kathleen tapped timidly on my door while I was fixing my hair. She came in to show me her dress and ribbons. She looked like she should have been on a calendar. Her pretty clothes and careful grooming accented her pixie-like quality. Her eyes sparkled as she caressed the lace on her pinafore.

"Do you like it?"

"It's lovely."

"Mama made it."

"She did?"

"She did," she nodded.

"It's beautiful. Your mama is a very fine seamstress."

"That's what Papa says."

She then studied me. "You look nice, too. Did you make your dress?" I shook my head, thinking of the shop in Toronto where the dress had been purchased.

"No," I said slowly, "Madame Tanier made it."

"She's good, too," Kathleen said solemnly.

I smiled, thinking of the madame and her prices. Yes, she was good, too.

The church building was new, though not as large as the one I had been used to attending. The people were friendly, and it was easy to feel at home, especially because I came as Jon's sister. It was plain to see that they regarded Jon and Mary with a great deal of respect.

I sat between William and Sarah. It was difficult for William not to squirm. He shifted this way, then that, swung this foot, then the other, made fists, then relaxed them. I couldn't help but feel sorry for him. Kathleen did not fare much better than William. Sarah, on the other hand, sat quietly. At one point, when we stood to sing a hymn, she slipped a little hand into mine. I gave it a squeeze and smiled at her. She cuddled up to me like a little puppy.

After the service was over I was introduced to a number of the people. The congregation was made up mostly of young couples, though I did see several men who seemed to be unattached. I appreciated the fact that Jon did not steer me in their direction. He left me with Mary and a few of her friends and went over to greet the men by himself.

The minister, his wife and four children were invited to join us at Jon and Mary's for Sunday dinner. The Reverend Dickson had come west three years ago. He wanted to talk of nothing but the West and was full of glowing accounts of the great things that were happening all around him. Mrs. Dickson was eager to discuss anything and everything about "back home." I felt much like a tennis ball during the conversation.

The next day Jon and Mary invited Mr. Higgins, the district's school superintendent, for dinner.

I was anxious to meet Mr. Higgins and to find out about my new school, but I was nervous about it too. What if he didn't feel that I could do a proper job? A man with his great responsibility, who was conscientiously searching for just the right teachers for his needy schools, could be extremely fussy about whom he chose to fill those needs.

I pictured Mr. Higgins as a rather reserved and learned man, balding, maybe a bit overweight, carefully clothed and austere. His bearing, his manner, his very look would speak the seriousness with which he regarded his responsibilities.

When Sarah announced that Mr. Higgins had arrived, I hastened to the parlor, pausing at the doorway to compose myself for this important meeting. I was not prepared for what I saw.

At first, I must confess, my eyes searched the room for a third party; I was certain that the gentleman laughing and joking with Jon was not, nor could *possibly* be, School Superintendent Higgins. But while my gaze traveled round the room, Jon turned and introduced his guest as Mr. Higgins.

The man was rather young—about thirty-five, I guessed. He was not carefully groomed, nor was he dignified or austere. His appearance and his conversation indicated to me that he was sloppy, loud, arrogant, and bold. I didn't like any of those things in a man.

I felt an inner check, quickly reminding myself that one must never make snap judgments based on first impressions. Even so, it was difficult for me to smile politely and extend my hand, but I did. Higgins nearly broke my fingers as he pumped a generous, manly handshake. He boomed out, "How d'ya do? How d'ya do?"

He didn't say that he was pleased to meet me, but I got the feeling that he was, for his eyes carelessly passed over my face and form. He seemed to approve, for he kept right on staring at me. I felt the color creeping into my face. Brother Jon came to my rescue.

"Let's be seated," he said. "I'm sure that Miss Thatcher is anxious to find out all about our school district."

Mentally I thanked Jon for using my formal name. Perhaps that would keep the forward Mr. Higgins at bay.

I voiced agreement with Jon. "Yes, I'm most interested in everything concerning the schools of this area, in particular the one that I will be serving."

"Later!" thundered Higgins. "I never spoil a good dinner by discussing mundane things like work before I eat."

He laughed loudly at what he considered his wit and turned to ask my impression of the West. I could tell by his voice that he felt there was nothing, anywhere, that could in any way come near to equalling *his* West. I replied that I had been in the West such a very short time that I really hadn't had a proper chance for evaluation. I wasn't sure that he accepted my statement. I sensed that he felt one shouldn't need time to clearly see the West's superiority. But instead of contradicting me, he said something about "showing me around." Jonathan again rescued me by steering the conversation to other subjects, and it wasn't long until Mary announced that dinner was served.

The roast beef was delicious. I would have loved the opportunity to enjoy it, but Mr. Higgins spoiled it for me. His open stare followed my every move, and I felt so nervous that I could scarcely direct my fork properly. I had never met such a man before, and I mentally conceded that I had finally met my first bore. So puffed up was he with importance and his own opinions that he monopolized and manipulated the entire conversation. My first impression had been correct: I did not care for Mr. Higgins, School Superintendent. Hopefully, all of the men in the West were not like this man.

We never did discuss the school system, though it seemed like hours and hours before he finally had sense enough to excuse himself and go home. As he prepared to leave, he asked if he could call again.

"Well," I said, hoping that he would catch my meaning in the tone of my voice, "we do need to talk about the school that I am to teach, and I need to find out what I will require. We haven't found *time* for that yet."

He guffawed as if I was delightful and squeezed my hand as he shook it. I pulled away.

"I'll see you Wednesday," he said, and he winked. I was shocked at his brazen manner and a little gasp of surprise escaped me. He didn't notice it, and bawled a merry "good-night" that I was afraid might awaken the sleeping children, then went whistling down the walk.

"Someone should marry that man and polish him up a bit," Mary said softly.

I shook my head and said, "It will take more than polish. I would not impose such a task on *any* woman."

On Tuesday Jon decided that I should be introduced to Calgary's shops, so he drove me downtown and left me while he went to his office. Mary had planned to accompany us, but William had an earache so she stayed with him.

The shops were certainly different from what I had been used to. I didn't see any that would compare with Madame Tanier's, but I did find them all most interesting. How I wished that Julie were with me. What fun we could have had!

Jon had promised to meet me for lunch at a nearby hotel, and as twelve o'clock approached I felt hungry. I decided to make my way to the dining room he had pointed out earlier. As I moved down the sidewalk, I was aware of many stares that followed me. I felt a small nervous twisting in my stomach. Perhaps it was unacceptable for a lady to walk alone in Calgary. I would have to ask Jonathan. I hurried my steps.

The Calgary streets were alive with variety. Besides the dark-suited businessmen, there were ranchers, farmers, Indians, and just plain loafers. I caught my breath and hurried past a rough-cut foursome who slouched against a hardware store. I could hear remarks and laughs, but I did not try to untangle any of the comments. I had no desire to know if they concerned me.

When I reached the hotel dining room, Jon was already there, ten minutes ahead of the appointed time.

"I didn't want you to arrive before me and have to stand around alone and wait," he said. I deeply appreciated his thoughtfulness.

We were led to a table, and as we moved through the room Jon greeted many acquaintances. For some parties he stopped and introduced me, to others he only nodded his greeting and called them by name. I began to see the pattern. When Jon stopped and made an introduction, it was always to a couple or to a married man. Jon would then make reference to Mr.—, who with his wife and family lived on such-and-such a street, or operated such-and-such a business. The gentlemen that he bypassed were obviously single. Jon was keeping his word and making no effort to pair me off. I smiled to myself at his obvious attempt to comply with my wishes.

As I sat down I could see and feel stares following me. I laid aside my gloves and purse and smiled at my brother. I hoped that pretending to be at ease would make me feel less edgy. It worked at least in part. Jon took over and soon I felt quite relaxed, even in my new surroundings. I was becoming quite attached to my brother. It was no wonder Mother idolized him. I wished that she could see him here, in this town with his lovely wife and well-behaved children, with his prestigious position in the community. She would be so proud. I also felt proud as I sat opposite him, and momentarily I was able to forget the stares.

"By the way," he said cautiously, "your clothes are lovely. Mary thinks so too. But Mary—well—even though she envies you, she—well—she has suggested that I hint, tactfully, that you should maybe have a few things a bit more practical for school teaching. Our classrooms are not all that fancy, and, well—I'm not good at hinting so . . ."

I laughed. Jon looked relieved.

"Whew," he said, "I'm glad that you took it that way. I wasn't sure whether you'd be annoyed or hurt. I'm just no good at beating 'round-the-bush. But Mary *is* right; your high-fashion clothing looks marvelous, but it's not too practical for our way of living."

Jon's sincerity and sweetness took any sting out of his words. I realized that he and Mary were right; it was love that prompted them to suggest the change in wardrobe.

"I'll see what I can find," I promised, as our food arrived.

"By the way," I ventured, "is it improper for a lady to venture out without an escort on Calgary streets?"

"Why? Didn't you meet any ladies this morning?"

"Yes—yes, I did, come to think of it. Several. But—"

Jon frowned.

"Well, I just felt out-of-place. Wherever I went, people stared."

Jon grinned.

"People—or men?"

I flushed. There was no need to continue the conversation.

Jonathan suggested some shops where I might find the type of clothing suitable for a western schoolmarm, and promised that he would meet me at three o'clock to drive me home. At first I thought there would be no pleasure in shopping for things that I considered drab and unstylish, but the more I looked the more I liked what I found, and the more fun it became. Again I wished for Julie's company. She would have turned the shopping trip into a hilarious occasion.

I found some simple cotton gowns that would be easy to wash and iron, and some undergarments without much lace. I even purchased heavier stockings; though, I must admit, I didn't care much for the looks of them. I had the clerk bundle up my purchases and checked the time. It was already past three o'clock. I hurried from the store, concerned that Jon might be waiting.

He was there, just a few steps down the street, his broad back turned to me. I hurried toward him and then noticed that he was in conversation with another man. I hesitated. Should I make my presence known in case Jon was in a hurry to get home, or should I wait until he had finished his conversation?

They shifted their position somewhat. I now could see the gentleman to whom Jon was talking. He was a bit taller than Jon, which made him tall indeed. A broad-brimmed hat shaded his eyes, but I noticed a strong, though not stubborn, jaw, and a well-shaped nose. He had a clear, clean-cut look, though one would certainly never consider him a "parlor-gentleman." There was a certain masculine ruggedness about him that suggested confidence and capability. He smiled good-naturedly as he spoke with Jon, and I imagined an easy friendliness and an appreciation for a good joke.

My slight movement must have caught his eye, for his head lifted. This caused Jon to look around.

"Be right with you, Beth," he said, and they shook hands heartily. "Greet Phillip for us," Jon said as he placed a hand on the man's shoulder. In return Jon received a friendly slap on the back; then the man turned to me. He nodded slightly, raising his hat as he did so, allowing me a full look into his eyes. They were deep blue—and determined; but they gave a glint of humor now, even though his lips did not move. I found myself wishing to see him smile, truly smile, but before I could offer one to encourage him, he turned and strode away.

I could not understand the strange stirring within me. I

suddenly wished that Jon had broken his rule and introduced us. Never before had I seen a man who interested me so much. I stood staring after him like a schoolgirl.

"A—a friend?" I stammered, and then blushed at my foolishness. Surely Jon would think me silly; it would have been apparent to anyone that they were friends.

"Yes."

That was all my brother said. No offering of the man's name or where he was from—nothing. I determined not to pursue the matter.

The next day Mr. Higgins showed up a bit after two o'clock. I was hoping that he was ready to get down to business, but he wanted to take me for a drive instead. I went, reluctantly. The whole thing was annoying, and I was very glad that I had a dinner engagement that evening and could insist that I must be home in plenty of time to prepare for it.

I pressed him about the school where I would be teaching, but he said that he was still undecided. I reminded him that I should know soon so that I could make adequate preparations. He continued to be evasive. I noted that there was only a week until classes would commence. He replied heartily that a lot could happen in a week, then exploded in an uproarious laugh. I dropped the subject.

He left me at the door and remarked how quickly the afternoon had passed. He asked if he could see me on Friday. Helplessly, I replied that since it was imperative that I know my future plans, he could. He boldly put a hand on my arm as he shook my hand. "Oh, I do have plans, my dear," he said. "I do have plans for you."

The nerve of him, I thought, as I climbed the stairs to my room. Never had I met such an obnoxious man. And to think that I was in a position where he would be my employer! I did hope that our respective duties would rarely bring us into contact with one another.

Suddenly the face of Jon's friend came to mind. *What a shame that he didn't turn out to be Mr. Higgins,* I thought, but immediately scolded myself. How foolish to even think such ridiculous thoughts!

But I was amazed at the intensity of my feelings. I had seen the man only once for just a moment. Why should he affect me so? I didn't know, but those blue smiling eyes stayed with me, to haunt me as I opened the door to my room. With a great deal of determination I pushed the image of the face from my mind and concentrated on choosing a gown for the evening ahead.

SEVEN

Mr. Higgins' Plan

Mr. Higgins arrived at eleven o'clock on Friday. I was reading to Sarah and Kathleen and was totally unprepared for such an early call. He rudely barged his way through the house and declared that we were going on a picnic. He carried a picnic basket as evidence that everything was prepared. I tried to stammer a refusal, but he cut me short with a laugh.

"You needn't bother your pretty little head about a thing. I know that I've surprised you—but folks will tell you that I'm full of surprises."

He seemed to consider people's comments regarding his surprises as great compliments.

He grabbed my hand and pulled me to my feet, not even letting me finish the final half of the last page.

"Come—come," he said. "Picnics don't like to be kept waiting."

"I like picnics," Kathleen announced hopefully.

"And someday your aunt and I will take you with us—but not today. Today is a picnic for just *two.*" He turned to me with a wink. "Now run along, my dear, and put on something more suitable for a picnic." He glanced at my stylish slippers. "Especially on your feet," he added. "Those flimsy little things are hardly suitable for a walk in the country, and we must have peace and quiet to discuss your future."

I hurried upstairs and changed, muttering threats the whole time. I chose the plainest of the dresses that I had purchased in Calgary; but I wished with all of my heart that I had something made out of floursacking to wear instead. I searched through the closet for the walking shoes I had used for the classroom and put them on. *They're awfully plain—almost ugly,* I thought, but I was glad of it as I descended the stairs.

Mr. Higgins, I thought, *today you will tell me where I am to teach—or so help you . . .*

I stepped onto the front porch where my caller was waiting, gathered a light shawl from the porch swing, fastened my least becoming hat in place, and reluctantly turned to the impatient Mr. Higgins who sighed loudly with relief.

His gaze then swept over me, both complimenting and criticizing me.

"You won't need the hat. The sun will feel good—"

"A lady does not leave the house without her hat," I retorted.

"Here in the West—"

"*I* am of the East."

He howled as though I had made a hilarious joke. But he quickly forgot about the hat as his eyes fell to my shoes.

"Those shoes—" he said next, "how will you ever walk in them? They are much too—"

"Mr. Higgins," I cut in, "I am beginning to have doubts about accompanying you. If these shoes will not do, then I must question where you are about to take me."

He dropped the matter of my attire and offered me his arm. I pretended not to notice and proceeded down the walk on my own to a rather nice-looking buggy and horse.

Mr. Higgins made a great affair of pointing out to me the fall colors, and I would have enjoyed them had I been with any other company. I did miss the deep reds of the oak and maple I had known at home, but my spirit drank in the gold of the shivering poplar mixed with the green shades of pine and spruce in the river valley. It truly was breathtaking.

Mr. Higgins drove west out of the city. A hill rose directly ahead of us, and I knew that if we topped it, we'd see those glorious mountains. But I did not want to see the mountains with

Mr. Higgins. I was deeply relieved when he stopped just short of the brow of the hill.

He leaped from the buggy and came around the horse to me, reaching a hand up to help me down. I could not refuse it without being dreadfully rude, but I pulled away from him as quickly as I was settled on the ground. He found a spot that suited him and spread out a rug and then the picnic things. Happily, the food was good. We talked about this and that; but remembering his comment about withholding business discussion until after one had eaten, I did not try to steer the conversation toward my teaching position. But I was determined that as soon as the meal was cleared away, I would broach the subject, if Mr. Higgins didn't bring it up himself.

As soon as he had finished eating, he stood up.

"Come, my dear," he said, holding out his hand.

I wished that he wouldn't use such a familiar term in addressing me. It unnerved me.

"Come," he said again. "I want to show you something."

I waved my hand toward the scattered remains of our lunch. "But the—"

"That'll keep. We'll pack it up when we come back," he said, unconcerned.

"By then the ants and flies—"

"My, my, you are a fussy thing, aren't you?" He sounded near exasperation, so I turned my back on the rug and its contents. After all, it was his basket, and if he didn't mind taking home a colony of ants, why should I?

We walked up the side of the grassy hill. I could see now why he had been concerned about my shoes. There was no path up the steep slope, and the walking was difficult. He offered his hand whenever I slowed a bit, so I hurried on ahead of him. By the time he called a halt, I was out of breath and glad to stop.

He reached out and turned me slowly so that I could look back upon the autumn-painted valley. The river and the town stretched out before us. From our vantage point the buildings of Calgary looked sheltered and protected. I tried to pick out Jon and Mary's house but couldn't find it.

"I've got something to say." There was excitement and a note of confidence in Mr. Higgins' voice.

"My school—you've decided. . . ?"

He laughed that hearty, grating laugh of his. I turned to look at him, uncharitably noticing the wrinkles in his suit.

"This property—right where we're standing—it's mine. I just bought it."

I blinked, unable to comprehend any connection between what Mr. Higgins had just said and any possible interest of mine. Then, remembering my manners, I offered, "Why, that's very nice. I'm happy for you. You certainly have picked a nice view. What do you plan—?"

"I'm going to build my house—right here—with a full, clear look at the valley."

I looked back down the valley. "Very nice," I commented rather absentmindedly.

"Do you really like it?"

"Why, yes. Yes, of course. It's lovely." I hoped that I hadn't tried to overdo it. It *was* lovely, but I really didn't feel that much enthusiasm.

"I knew that you would." The confidence was in his voice again. "We'll put the house right here," he said, waving his arm.

Noticing the "we," a sympathy for whoever the other member was swept through me, along with a slight thankfulness that even a man like Mr. Higgins could find someone with whom to share life.

"We'll face this way—the front entry, the living room . . ." he said, making grand gestures with his arm. "What do you think?"

I couldn't imagine why he was asking me, but I mumbled that I supposed that would be just fine.

"I think that we'll build of brick rather than lumber, though lumber is easier to get. Four or five bedrooms, do you think?"

"Mr. Higgins, I—"

"You don't need to call me Mr. Higgins, my dear Beth," he said ingratiatingly. I was shocked at his liberty in using my first name. "It's Thomas—Tom, if you like—" his eyes were filled with feeling as he looked at me, "or anything else you'd care to call me."

"Mr. Higgins," I stubbornly repeated his formal name. "I'm afraid that I don't understand. We came here to discuss my school, and instead—"

"Ah, my dear. I see that I haven't made myself clear. You won't need to take a teaching position. We can be married soon and I—"

"Married?" My reply sounded almost like a shriek. "Married? What are you speaking of?"

"Don't be coy, my dear. I see no need for waiting. Some may think it a bit hasty, but here in the West a man is given the privilege of deciding quickly. There is no need to wait just for convention's sake. The marriage—"

"But I came west to *teach*!"

"Of course," he said knowingly, "until such time as a suitable—"

"Mr. Higgins, I don't think that you understand." I took a deep breath to calm myself. "There were 'suitable' men back East. I have no intention of forsaking teaching to—to marry—to marry *you*!"

It was several minutes before I convinced Mr. Higgins that I meant what I said. He couldn't believe that any woman in her right mind would actually reject his offer—so you can readily see how he, henceforth, rated me. With disgust he abruptly turned to descend the slope ahead of me, and I was hard put to keep up with him. Without another word between us, he jammed leftovers, dishes, ants and all into his picnic basket, piled it all into the buggy, and we drove back to Jon's in awkward silence.

"Remember," he finally grated out as we neared my brother's place, "I am the school superintendent. I hire and I fire."

"Perhaps you would rather I returned to the East. I'll just tell Jonathan—"

"How absurd," he cut in. "We've plenty of schools where teachers are needed. I'm sure that I'll be able to find a spot suitable for you."

"Thank you," I said stiffly. "That *is* why I came."

The appointment came by letter. The note was short and formal. After careful consideration, it stated, I was to be given the Pine Springs school. Enclosed was a train ticket which I was to use the next Wednesday. The train would take me to Lacombe where I would be met by Mr. Laverly, the local school-board chairman. I would have the remaining days to get settled before classes commenced on the following Monday.

"Lacombe," I said aloud. "Where is Lacombe?"

"North," said Jon from behind his paper. "Why?"

"That's where I'm to go."

The paper went down and Jon's face appeared.

"Go? For what?"

"My school."

"That can't be."

"It's right here—even a train ticket."

"But it's—it's more than a hundred miles from here. That can't be."

"Over a hundred?"

"Right. There must be some mistake."

It hit me then. Mr. Higgins was seeing to it that I was a long way removed from Calgary. His revenge? Perhaps he was even hoping that I would refuse the placement and go whimpering back east. Well, I wouldn't.

"I'm sure that there's no mistake, Jon," I said evenly. "It sounds delightful."

"You mean you'd consider—"

"Of course."

"Lacombe, eh?"

"No, actually it's called Pine Springs."

"It's way out in the country!"

"Sounds delightful," I said again.

"It's backwoods, barely opened up. I'm sure there's been a mistake. I'll talk to Thomas."

"No, Jon, please," I said quickly. "I want to take it."

At the startled and hurt look in Jon's eyes I hurried to explain. "Oh, I'll hate to leave you, and Mary, and the children. I've learned to love you all so, but really, it'll be good for me. Can't you see? I've been so sheltered, so—so coddled. I'd like to find out if I can care for myself, if I can stand on my own two feet."

"You're sure?" Jon looked at my carefully groomed hair, my soft hands and manicured nails, at my stylish clothes.

I understood his look. "I'm sure," I said emphatically.

"Well, I don't know what Mother will think. You were supposed to be under my protective wing."

"Mother won't need to know—yet."

"But—"

"She'll know that I am on my own, certainly, but as to the distance between us, that would only worry her unnecessarily."

"I'm still not convinced, but if you think—"

"Oh, I do. I really want to try it, Jon."

Jon's newspaper went back up to indicate that he considered the issue closed. I sat very still and fingered the ticket to Lacombe.

"Say, I just thought of something," said Jon, coming out from behind his paper again. "Pine Springs—that's Wynn's country."

"Who?"

"Wynn, the fellow that you saw me talking to the other day when you did your shopping. Remember?"

Did I remember! I tried to sound very nonchalant. "Oh, yes, I believe I recall the one you mean. He's not from Calgary?"

"Not really. He comes and goes. He was in that day visiting his brother Phillip. Phillip's been in the hospital here."

"Oh, I see."

I could feel the excitement flowing through my veins, warming my cheeks. I was glad that Jon was behind his paper again.

I gathered up my short letter and my now-welcome train ticket and muttered something about beginning my packing, then headed for my room.

So Jon's friend Wynn was from Pine Springs. Perhaps when I reached Pine Springs I would have the pleasure of meeting him. Jon had not introduced me to him, even though he had been given the perfect opportunity. If I understood my brother's little code, this meant that Wynn was single. I smiled softly.

You silly goose! I scolded myself. *You're acting in a manner that even Julie would declare to be childish. Stop this nonsense this minute! I honestly don't know what has come over you.*

Still, I couldn't help but whisper as I fingered the train ticket, "Thank you, Mr. Thomas Higgins."

EIGHT

The New School

The time drew near for my trip to Lacombe, and I felt both excited and sad. I would miss my newly found family; Jon and Mary had become very dear to me, and the children were all so special. William hovered nearby to see how he might help, and Sarah looked ready to cry the entire time that she watched me pack. Kathleen insisted upon helping me fold the green emerald velvet as I returned it to its tissues; she expressed her sorrow that I hadn't even worn it during my stay.

I held Baby Elizabeth for the last time, and she gave me the most endearing smile. I kissed her soft dimpled cheeks and a tear or two trickled down my own.

Mary was forever reminding me that I would be welcome in their home at any time. "Please," she begged, "come whenever you can, even if it's only for overnight."

I promised that I would try.

"And should you find—"

"Everything will be fine, I'm sure." I knew that she was giving me an invitation to flee back to her if I found my situation unsuitable. I appreciated her concern, but I didn't want to be a baby. I suppose, too, that I wanted to show Mr. Higgins a thing or two!

"But you never know what kind of a family you will be boarding with," Mary suggested, her voice hesitant.

"I'm sure that they wouldn't place me in an objectional home," I said, trying to sound confident. In truth, I had little faith in Mr. Higgins' concern for my well-being. I did not know how far he might go in gaining revenge.

"But remember . . ." Mary said, and I assured her that I would.

Jon drove me to the train, and William, Sarah and Kathleen rode along. Kathleen, very serious, asked me, "Aunt Beth, will you 'member me if I grow up while you're gone?"

"Of course I will, sweetheart," I assured her. "But I'm not going to stay away nearly as long as that."

She seemed comforted by my reply.

"Wish you were gonna be *my* teacher," William pouted.

"Me, too," Sarah echoed with great feeling. She was to begin school the next Monday and, though she was looking forward to it, she had some fears also.

"So do I," I said, hugging them. "But I promise I'll write and tell you all about Pine Springs and my pupils there, and you can write me about your new teachers and friends."

They brightened at the thought of a letter.

After the final good-byes, I boarded the train and chose what I hoped would be a comfortable seat. A cigar-puffing man across the aisle made me realize that I had chosen unwisely, but I was reluctant to move for fear of appearing rude. His wife finally demanded that he put out his cigar; she couldn't stand the closeness of the "foul-smellin' stuff." I was delivered.

I thought that the train would never reach Lacombe. We limped along, stopping at any place with more than one building. The train hissed and coughed and shuttled and groaned, seemingly forever, at these tiny train stations before finally rolling on.

We spent an especially long time at a town called Red Deer. I watched with interest as dray wagon after dray wagon drove away with loads of freight—sacks of flour, unmarked crates, even a stove. At last, when I was sure that they must have removed even *my* luggage, we resumed our forward crawl.

The landscape had changed over the miles. We had left the prairies behind and now rolled through timbered land. Here and there were fields where settlers had cleared the land for the plow. Large piles of logs and stumps were scattered about, some of them surrounded by planted grain.

The crops that had been sown were now nearly ready for

harvest, and much of the talk of my fellow passengers was centered on yield, quality, and the weather. It was conversation unfamiliar to me, and I found myself listening intently.

It was well into the afternoon before the conductor came through calling, "Lacombe! Next stop, Lacombe."

I began to bundle together the items that I had brought with me. I carefully tucked away the wrappings of the lunch that Mary had insisted upon sending. I had been most reluctant to comply at the time she suggested it, but I was now glad that she hadn't allowed me to talk her out of it. I had eaten every morsel of the lunch and been thankful for it. I brushed at my lap for unseen crumbs and stood to my feet to smooth my skirt.

The train squealed to a jerky halt. I clutched my belongings and went forward to meet Mr. Laverly. Stiff and bedraggled after only these few hours on the train, I had difficulty imagining how I had endured the four days it had taken me to journey from Toronto.

As I descended the steps, my eyes searched hastily about for a man that looked like a Laverly. I easily spotted the one who had been sent to meet me; he was the *other* nervous person on the platform. I introduced myself, and he suggested that I might like a cup of coffee before we started out. He would stay and load my belongings. His daughter, Pearlie, was pushed forward with instructions to be my guide to the local hotel tearoom. I was glad to fall in step with Pearlie. The hotel was only a short distance, and she led me at a brisk pace.

We found a table in the corner, and after we had placed our orders and I had caught my breath, we began to chat. I was pleased to find that Pearlie was not shy and offered information freely. I was anxious to discover any information I could about Pine Springs.

"How do you like school?" I asked, thinking that this would be a normal question for a teacher to ask.

"Fine, but I didn't like my last teacher good as the one before. But," she hurried on, after a quick check of my response to that, "least he was better than the one 'fore that."

"Do you have a new teacher every year?"

"Most of the time. One I had for a year an' a half once."

She shrugged it off as of no consequence.

"How far is Pine Springs?"

"Pa says it'll take 'bout half an hour."

"What's it like?"

"Don't know. Never been there before."

My eyes must have opened wide at this reply.

"You don't live in Pine Springs?"

"Uh-uh. Live here in Lacombe."

"But I thought that it was your father who will be driving me to Pine Springs."

" 'Tis. Nobody in Pine Springs has got an auto, so Mr. Laverly hired my pa to drive you on out. Team takes a long time an' Mr. Laverly said that by the time you got there by horse an' wagon, you might decide to pack right up an' head on back East. An he sure didn't want that."

"I see." I smiled at Mr. Laverly's assessment of a lady from the East. "Then you aren't a Laverly."

"Nope. We're Ainsworths."

"You live and go to school here in Lacombe?"

"Yup."

"Do you have any idea how many children attend the Pine Springs school?"

"Never been any yet."

"Pardon me?"

"It's bran' new. They jest built it. They been tryin' to get a teacher, an' Mr. Higgins never had one for 'em. They built the school two years ago—an' no teacher. An' then last fall, no teacher. Now this year they get a teacher. Mr. Laverly sounded real excited. That's why he asked Pa to drive you out. My pa's 'bout the only one 'round here with a good auto," she added proudly.

"That's very nice. What does your father do?"

"He's an undertaker, an' business has been unusual good—I heard him tell Ma. Says that she can even have that new washing machine that she's been a'wantin'. Won't need to use the old scrub board no more."

I smiled and nodded. "That will be nice for your mother."

Pearlie watched me carefully. As soon as I had finished my tea, she rose from her chair.

"We best get back. Pa will be done loadin' your stuff."

"Are you going with us to Pine Springs?" I asked, hoping that she was.

"I gotta," she stated. "I gotta help Pa start the car."

"You help? What do you do?"

"I choke it an' things, whilst he cranks."

We walked back to the station and found Pearlie's pa pacing back and forth in an agitated fashion. Before him on the platform sat my trunks. I guessed by the look that the station master sent my way that he and Pearlie's pa had already had words. Without any preliminaries, Pearlie's father stated, "These'll have to stay. Got no place in my automobile for freight like thet."

"But I need them!" I protested. "They contain my clothing, my—"

"Can't do a thing 'bout thet. I can take the luggage thet you're a'carryin', but the trunks will have to stay here. Someone will jest have to come on in with a wagon an' pick 'em up."

I could see that his mind was made up. Besides, he appeared to be right. There was no room in the automobile for my trunks.

"I put yer other things on the backseat there. You can seat yerself there beside 'em."

I did as I was told. The station master was summoned with a wave and given instructions regarding my trunks. They were soon riding a cart into the small wooden building.

Pearlie took her place behind the steering wheel and expertly pulled and twisted knobs while her father began his cranking chore. It took a good deal of hard work before the automobile coughed into action. He came dashing from the front, through the door, and bumped Pearlie out of his way, his face red and sweaty from his exertion.

We began to chug our way carefully through the little town, avoiding potholes, pedestrians, and teams. Dogs took pleasure in chasing this unusual conveyance, teasing and barking and snapping at the tires as they escorted us out of town. I held my breath lest we hit one of them, but Pearlie's pa drove as though they were not even there.

It was a long, dusty, bumpy ride. The road certainly wasn't built for speeding, and Pearlie's father couldn't have been accused of doing so. But lest I sound ungrateful, I was glad that I didn't have to make this trip by wagon.

I looked for my beloved mountains, but from this vantage-point saw only tree-covered hills.

We passed several fields that had been cleared from the timbered countryside, many of them holding a grain crop in various stages of ripening. Some fields grazed cattle or horses, and I even saw a few sheep. Most of the homes and outbuildings were of log construction; I found them fascinating.

I was about to tap Pearlie on the shoulder and ask how much farther when I remembered that she wouldn't know either, having never been to Pine Springs before. About ten minutes later, we turned into a driveway and there stood a log building that I realized must be my school.

We drove on past it, across the browning grass, and pulled up before a smaller building to the left and rear of the school itself.

"Here we are," Pearlie's father called above the roar of the motor. It came to me that he did not plan to turn it off—he did not wish the unpleasant exertion of starting it again. I didn't blame him.

I must have shown my bewilderment, for he boomed at me, "The teacherage—where you'll be stayin'."

Teacherage? I got my thoughts and my baggage gathered together and crawled from the car. My companions did not leave their positions in the auto.

"I don't have a key!" I wailed through the auto's window.

"A key?"

He acted as if he had never heard of such an object.

"Yes, a key—to let myself in the house."

"Won't need no key. Doesn't have a lock. Good-day, ma'am." And he tipped his hat, pushed the shift lever into gear, and the auto clattered and chugged its way out of the yard.

I watched them go. Pearlie waved wildly, and I lifted my hand in a limp salute. When they had disappeared from sight, I gathered up my parcels and tried the door. Pearlie's pa had been right; it opened readily to my touch, and I entered what was now my new home.

I had fully expected that I would be a boarder in some neighborhood home. A funny little fear rippled through me. But I told myself not to be silly, that living alone would be much more to my liking and that I would be so close to my classroom.

I learned later that the teacherage had been constructed over the last winter as an added incentive to Mr. Higgins to provide the community with a teacher. I was its first occupant.

I passed through an entry into a small room which was a combined kitchen and living room. A bit of a cupboard stood in one corner and next to it was a very used stove. A fire was burning in it, so someone must have recently been in the teacherage. A teakettle sat on the stove and sent forth a merry, soft purr with its column of wavering steam. Something about that kettle suddenly made me feel much more at home. I felt myself relax. My eyes quickly glanced around the room. It also contained a table and two chairs, mended and freshly painted a pale green. Two stuffed chairs, with home-made crazy-quilt throws carefully covering them and a small table sitting between them, made my living room. A chest of sorts stood against one wall.

I could see into a second room, and after making a hurried survey of the first, I quickly passed through the adjoining door to get a better look. This room contained a bed and a dresser. The furniture looked worn, but clean. The bed's mattress looked lumpy, but a new cover had been sewn for it of freshly laundered floursacking. A brand-new pillow graced the spot where my head would rest;

I wondered if its soft downiness came from a neighbor's fowls. A colorful crazy quilt was folded neatly at the end.

Realizing I was still carrying my bags, I returned to the first room and tumbled them into one of the overstuffed chairs. In somewhat of a trance, I crossed to the stove and checked to see if it needed more wood. I had never taken care of a stove before and hadn't the slightest notion how to go about handling it, but it seemed fairly obvious as to where the wood should go.

I looked around me. There were some things set out on the table and I crossed over to them. A note caught my eye, and I stopped to read it.

> Dear Miss
>
> Thot that you'd be tired and hungry after yer trip so have left some things. We will call on you tomarra to see what you be needing. We hope you like it here. We are plenty glad to have you come.
>
> Martha Laverly

On the table sat containers of tea, sugar, coffee, and salt, as well as cheese, fresh bread, and pound cake. I crossed to the cupboard and opened the doors. A collection of mismatched dishes and pots greeted me. I lifted out a brown teapot with a chipped lid, a blue cup with a rose on the side, placed it on a pale yellow saucer, and set about brewing myself a cup of tea.

While the tea steeped, I opened the other cupboard door and found staple items in small containers. Never having spent much time in a kitchen, I was thankful to see that they were carefully labeled.

On the cupboard sat a pan filled with water and in the water stood three jars. One contained cream, another milk, and a third, butter. *So this is how one keeps things sweet when there is no icebox.* I poked a finger into the water and was surprised at how cool it felt.

The chest standing near the door held a pail of water with a small dipper, a basin, and a tin container with a bar of soap. I poured a little of the water into the basin and washed my hands.

Realizing that I had no towel on which to dry them until my trunks arrived, I went outside and shook the water from my hands and then walked back and forth, rubbing them lightly together until all the water had evaporated.

My tea was ready when I returned. I sliced a piece of the fresh bread and spread on the butter, then cut myself a generous portion of cheese. Crossing to the stuffed chair that wasn't holding my belongings, I sat down with my repast. How good the hot tea and the fresh bread tasted! I couldn't remember ever having a more enjoyable meal.

My mind was beginning to clear of its fog, and I studied my new quarters more critically. The windows had white, rather stiff-looking curtains. The table was covered with a white cloth of the same material, but it was decorated with cross-stitching. The walls were bare except for a calendar. The rugs on the floor were small, bright rounds against the plainness of the bare wood. The furniture was definitely all secondhand. As I looked at it, I wondered about those folks who had given it up in order that the new teacherage might be furnished. Had it been a sacrifice for them? I set down my empty cup and again went to the bedroom.

The curtains that hung there were of the same coarse material. Two more quilts were neatly folded and stacked on a wall shelf. They were all homemade, obviously pieced together from the better parts of worn-out garments. Skillfully and artistically done, they were very attractive to look at. I admired the handiwork and appreciated the time which had gone into them. Three rugs were scattered on the floor, one in front of the bed, one in front of the dresser, and the third at the door. A mirror hung on the wall, a crack running jaggedly across one bottom corner.

So I won't be boarding, I again told myself. *I'll be living completely on my own, in this little pioneer log house.*

I returned to the lumpy chair and poured a fresh cup of tea. I looked around at my small, secondhand nest, feeling deep respect for the people who had worked so hard and sacrificed so much to bring me here. The sense of near-panic left me and a warm kinship with these pioneers began to seep into my mind and emotions. I felt almost happy as I thought about my still-unknown neighbors. *I will love your children, and I will teach them to the very best of my ability,* I decided then and there.

I smiled to myself and sipped the hot tea, I said aloud, "Thank you, Mr. Higgins. You couldn't have given me a more pleasant situation."

It wasn't until I went to find a basin and more hot water to wash up my few dishes that I discovered the covered pot of stew simmering on the back of the stove. It smelled delicious as I lifted the cover and stirred it, and even though my hunger had been completely satisfied with bread and cheese, I couldn't refrain from dishing myself a small serving. It *was* delicious. The rest would be my dinner for tomorrow.

NINE

The Wilderness

I spent the remainder of the daylight in further exploration of my new domain. Besides the school (the door of which was firmly nailed shut) and the house, there was also a shed for the wood supply, a small barn and two outhouses, marked "Boys" and "Girls." A pump stood in the yard, and I realized that this was my water supply. Not being able to resist that handle, I tried it. It was a long time before the water made an appearance. When it finally did come and I pushed my hand under the stream of water, it was so cold that I shivered. I sat down on the small platform to catch my breath, touching my still-cold hand to my hot cheeks and forehead.

The yard that I surveyed certainly needed care, but then, of course, it had been unattended. The tall grass had recently been cut but had been left to lie, browning where it fell. It smelled musty and insects buzzed busily about it.

I peeked in one of the windows in the small school building and glimpsed some desks in various sizes and condition, a large, potbellied stove near the door, and a teacher's desk in front of a homemade blackboard.

I did not go back to the teacherage until the sun had retired for the night. The sunset was a splendid display. I wondered if it was showing off for my benefit or if it was often that spectacular. Rarely had I seen such a gorgeous scene; the riotous colors flamed out over the sky in shades that I had no words to describe. Birds sang their last songs of the day before tucking in for the night, and still the darkness hung back. *Now,* I thought, *I understand the word "twilight." It was created for just this time—in this land.*

The air began to cool, and the darkness did start its descent at last. I slowly began picking my way toward my small haven, wanting to sing aloud the song that reverberated in my heart, yet holding myself in check. This new world was so peaceful, so harmonious.

I was lingering by a window of the school building, taking one last fruitless peek into the dark interior, when a blood-curdling, spine-chilling howl rent the stillness of the evening hour. It seemed to tear through my veins, leaving me terrified and shaking. The scream had hardly died away when another followed, to be joined by another.

I came to life then. A wolf pack! And right in my very yard! They had smelled new blood and were moving in for the kill.

I sprang forward and ran for the door of my cabin, praying that somehow God would hold them back until I was able to gain entrance. My feet tangled in the new-mown grass and I fell to my hands and knees. With a cry I scurried madly on, not even bothering to regain my feet. The sharp stubble of the grass and weeds bit into the palms of my hands, but I crawled on. Another howl pierced the night.

"Oh, dear God!" I cried, and tears ran down my cheeks.

Howls seemed to be all around me now. Starting as a solo, they would end up in a whole chorus. What were they saying to one another? I was certain that they were discussing my coming end.

Somehow I reached the door and scrambled inside. I struggled to my feet and stood with my back braced against the flimsy wooden barrier. I expected an attack to come at any moment. I heard no sound of rushing padded feet, only sporadic howling. But Julie had said that western wolves were like that—catlike and noiseless, silently stealing up on their victims.

My eyes lifted to the windows. The windows! Would they challenge the glass?

I forced myself to leave the door, checking first for some kind of lock. There was one, of sorts, but it was only a hook and eye. Totally inadequate against a half-ton wolf.

Julie had said that they were huge animals, with eyes that glared an angry red, jaws that were set in a grin of malice, and hackles that bulged a foot around their neck, making them look much like sinister men in heavy, broad-collared beaver coats.

With trembling fingers I fastened the hook on the door and rushed into the kitchen. What would deter them? Perhaps if I hung quilts over the windows, the smell of my warm blood would not reach them so readily. What had Julie said? Fire. That was it—fire. Fire was about the only thing that would hold them back.

I rushed to the stove. It was cold and flameless.

"I must get a fire started—I must!" I sobbed, and began to throw paper and kindling into the firebox. I knew that these supplies had been left for my use the next morning, but I needed them *now.*

My fingers fumbled with the match as a new burst of howls split the air. They didn't sound any closer, but perhaps that was their strategy, just to throw their victims off guard. Maybe some of them were sitting back and howling while others stole in quietly to make the kill.

The paper finally began to flame, and I thrust the kindling carelessly on top of it. The hungry, newborn flames consumed it greedily. I placed the lid on the stove. To my dismay there was then no evidence of fire except for the small amount of warmth that was beginning to radiate from the black metal of the stove top.

"I can't cover it—I can't, or it will be no protection at all," I told myself.

I removed the lid again. The flames were robust now, and I fed them more wood.

Smoke began to seep into the room, and as I huddled over the stove, as close to the flames as I dared, I began to cough. I pulled the handkerchief from my skirt pocket and covered my mouth. It was then I realized that my dress was ripped and hanging limply about my waist. I had nearly severed the skirt from the bodice. It must have happened during my frantic crawling.

I continued to feed the fire and huddle over it, coughing and crying into the woodsmoke. Suddenly I realized that it had been several minutes since I had heard a wolf howl. Was it a trick? Had they moved on, or were they just coaxing me away from the flames? I now wished that I had studied more about the habits of the wilderness creatures, like Julie had insisted. It had been foolish of me to venture into the wilds unprepared. Why, I didn't even have a gun or know how to use one.

My pounding heart sounded loud in the new stillness. I heard an owl hoot a few times, then it too seemed to move on. Still, I remained by the fire, not even daring to move to the window to look outside.

A harvest moon soon hung in the sky. I could tell by the brightness that it was full and orange like an autumn pumpkin. I stayed where I was and, between fits of coughing, stared at the shadows surrounding the trees at the far side of the yard. I could see plainly through the window as the moon rose higher and higher in the sky, but though I watched until my eyes ached with the strain, I saw nothing move. And then, to my amazement, two deer moved fearlessly out of the shadows and into the open yard. They began to feed, unconcerned, upon the scattered, mown grass. This was my first encouragement. Surely the deer wouldn't walk out boldly if the wolf pack was still around. But could the wolves so conceal themselves that even the deer couldn't detect them? Downwind—wasn't that it? The killer stalked his prey from downwind. Was there a wind blowing? Again I strained my eyes and my ears, but not a leaf shivered; I could not even hear a flutter in the stillness of the night.

I continued to feed my fire. The smoke in the room was almost unbearable now. I could not afford to leave the lid off the stove a minute longer or I would surely suffocate. Even with my handkerchief and the hem of my dress over my nose and mouth, I could scarcely stand to breathe the air of the room. My eyes watered until my handkerchief was soaked.

What could I do? To close the lid meant that my fire could not be seen, but to open the lid meant that I would soon be driven from the cabin. Perhaps that was what the wolves were waiting for. Maybe they knew that I could not endure the smoke-filled room much longer. Maybe they were gathered around my door at this very instant, waiting for me to stagger from the house and into their waiting jaws. I replenished the fire and closed the lid.

The minutes ticked slowly by. It was a long time until I was brave enough to step away from the stove. I was still struggling with some way to insure survival. *The lamp,* I thought suddenly. *The lamp might do as a fire substitute.*

I fumbled in the darkened room until I found the lamp and the matches. When the small flame flickered up, I beheld a room blue with smoke. No wonder I was having trouble breathing.

I looked around the room in dismay. There was nothing available for my defense, and it was very late. No one at this hour would be going by on the road that ran by my door. I guessed that, according to where the moon now hung, the night was half over. I ached with tiredness and fear, and my hands and knees stung from their scratches and bruises. What could I do?

It suddenly dawned on me that there was *nothing* that I could do, and that it was foolish to pretend to defend myself.

I placed more wood in the stove, set my lighted lamp on the table by the window, and went to my bedroom. Somewhere in my few belongings I had a nightgown, but I didn't bother searching for it. I closed the curtain and slipped my torn and soiled dress over my head. I left it lying where it fell and dropped on top of it one of my petticoats. Still wearing the other, I moved to the bed and spread the quilt over it. I had never slept without sheets before, and under different circumstances it might have bothered me to do so. It did not bother me now. I was about to lower myself onto the bed when I remembered the clean floursacking over the mattress. I stopped only long enough to gather up the skirt of my crumbled dress and carefully wipe my hands and feet on it. Then I lay down and pulled the quilt right over my head.

"Lord," I prayed, "I've done all that I know to do. You'll have to take over now."

The stuffiness under the quilt was no better than the smoke of the room. I was soon forced to uncover my nose so that I might get some air. Somehow I managed to cough myself to sleep.

TEN
Lars

When I awakened the next morning, the sun was already high in the sky. I woke up coughing, and it took me a few minutes to regain my bearings and realize what had happened. One glimpse of my garments lying in a heap on the floor, and it all came back to me.

The panic-stricken fear was gone. Julie had informed me also that wolves do not prowl around in broad daylight. I pushed back the quilt and moved my feet to leave my bed; stiffness and pain stopped me. I was instantly reminded of my bruised knees and realized that I should have properly cared for them before retiring. I slowly sat up and pulled up my petticoat to examine my wounds. The scratches were red and swollen but none appeared to be deep. A few days of healing would be all that was needed. I turned over my hands and looked at them, and found the same to be true. But I was shocked at their filthiness. Dirt-streaked and soot-smudged, I shuddered to think that I had actually gone to bed in such condition.

Crawling slowly and painfully out of bed, I limped around to open all of my windows in an effort to clear out the stubbornly clinging smoke. Then I washed myself as thoroughly as I could in cold water and dried myself on the cleanest portion of my soiled dress.

My scratches stung as I soaked the dirt out of them with the bar of soap and patted them dry. I wished that I had been sensible enough to bring some kind of ointment with me. Having none, I decided to try a small amount of cream from that jar that had been provided for my table. It did soothe the cuts some. I dressed rather stiffly and did the best I could with my hair. It was badly in need of a good washing after my dusty trip in the Ainsworths' automobile and the smoke of the previous night.

I had barely put things in order, built my fire and put on the coffeepot when there came a knock on my door. I had just prepared myself for a trip to the woodshed to replenish my wood supply. I had burned almost all of it from the big wooden box by my kitchen stove in my efforts to keep the wolves from my door. *My, it must take a lot of wood to get the folks around here through the winter—with the wolves and the constant blizzards and all,* I was thinking when the knock came.

I opened the door, and there stood a young boy whom I judged to be eight or nine. He was dressed in patched denim trousers and a freshly pressed cotton shirt. His blond hair was rather unruly, but his freckled face shone from its early morning washing.

"Hello," he said, a shy grin trying to get past his wary eyes.

"Hello," I answered, so glad to see him that I could have hugged him. He must have read the pleasure in my face, for his grin broke forth.

"Come in," I welcomed him with a smile of my own. "I'm Miss Thatcher."

He stepped forward awkwardly, timidly looked around for a moment, and then decided that he'd better get down to business.

"Ma sent me over to see if I could help ya none." His words were thick with a Scandinavian accent.

Some, my teacher's mind corrected, but I let it pass.

"That's very kind," I said.

"I can carry yer vood an' vater an' t'ings," the boy continued. Then he stopped and sniffed. "Smoky," he stated simply. "Havin' trouble vid yer fire?"

"It'll clear soon," I assured him, not wanting to blame the dependable old stove, but not knowing just how to bring up the matter of the wolves, either.

The aroma of the coffee made my stomach gurgle.

"Before you start on the wood and water, would you like to join me for breakfast?"

"T'ank ya, but I already haf my breakfast."

"Then make this a lunch," I suggested, and the boy laughed.

"Just sit down," I pointed toward the pale green chairs. "Take your pick."

He stepped to the nearest one and sat down. I spread four slices of bread with butter and strawberry preserves, poured milk for him and coffee for me, and joined him at the table. I bowed my head and said a short grace; his eyes showed no surprise. The bread and jam were delicious, and he seemed to enjoy them as much as I did.

"Yer lamp is still burnin'," he said suddenly. In the light of day I had failed to notice it. The wick had burned down so that only a tiny flame showed. I felt my cheeks flush in embarrassment, but without further comment the boy leaned over and blew out the struggling flame.

I wondered just how to start our conversation so that we might get to know one another. But he took care of that problem.

"I live on da farm yust over dere," he began, pointing a finger toward the northeast. "Vasn't fer da trees, you could see our house an' barn real plain."

This was good news. I had no idea that I had neighbors so near.

"Will you be one of my new pupils?"

"Ya mean, vill I go to school?"

"That's right."

"Me an' my sisters, Else an' Olga, an' my broder, Peter."

"That's nice," I said and really meant it. "And what is your name?"

"Lars—Lars Peterson. I vas named after my grandfader."

I could tell by the way he said it that he was proud of the fact.

"And your father's name?"

"Henry Peterson. An' Ma is Anna."

"And what class will you be in, Lars?"

"Don't know yet. Never been to school, but Pa has tried to teach us some letters an' some vords. Ma doesn't know da English vords too good yet. Pa studied a little bit in English ven he first came over. Ma came six mont's later vid us young-uns, an' she didn't haf time to study. But she knows numbers real good. Numbers ain't much different in any country, I guess."

I nodded and smiled, but I was thinking about the shame of a child nearing ten without ever having been in a classroom.

"I vas pretty little yet ven ve came from da old country." Lars continued. "Olga vas not t'ree yet and da tvins yust babies."

"How old are they now?"

"Olga is seven and a half, an' Else an' Peter are yust turned six."

"And you?"

"I'm nine."

He wiped the last crumbs from his cheeks and arose from the chair.

"I best be carryin' dat vood," he said, "yer almost out." I was relieved that he made no comment on the extraordinary amount I had used. "T'ank ya fer da good break—lunch," he finished with a grin. "I'll git ya some fresh vater first."

I moved to get him my water pail, pouring what still remained into the reservoir on the stove.

"Lars," I said slowly. I had to know, yet hardly knew how to ask, "What do people around here do about the wolves?"

"Volves?" He looked surprised and confused. Then he answered confidently, "Ve don't got no volves."

"But last night I heard them. And if your farm is so near, you should have heard them, too."

"Oh, dem. Dem's coyotes."

"Coyotes?"

"Yah, yust silly ole coyotes. Pa says dat coyotes are yella-livered. Scared of der own shadows, dey are. Von't even take on anyt'ing bigger dan a hen or a mouse."

"But they sounded—"

"Don't dey make a racket!" His eyes sparkled. "I like to listen to 'em. Dey sound so close-like, an' dey all howl togeder an—"

"Yes, they do sound close," I put in, shivering at my recollection. "And they never attack people?"

"Naw, not coyotes. Dey're scared silly of everyt'ing—especially people. Dey run vid der tails 'tveen der legs. I tried to sneak up on 'em a coupla times to get a good look at 'em, but soon as you git a little close, dey turn tail an' run off, slinkin' avay as fast as dey can go."

I felt relieved and embarrassed as I thought of my terror during the night I had just endured. Coyotes—harmless, noisy coyotes! Humiliation flushed my cheeks.

Lars suddenly turned to me, the empty water pail still in his hand.

"Miss T'atcher, ya know vat? Ven I vas little, I vas scared of 'em. I used to lay in bed vid my head under da covers, sveat-in' and cryin'." He blushed slightly. "Den my pa told me 'bout dem bein' sissies. Dey'd be more scared dan me if ve met up sudden. Pa says he's gonna git a coupla good dogs, yust to keep da coyotes avay from da chickens—chickens be 'bout da only t'ings dat need fear coyotes." He turned to go, then turned back. "Ya von't tell, vill ya—dat I used to be scared of silly coyotes?"

"No, I won't tell, No one will know—you can be sure," I promised him. He left the room with relief showing in his eyes.

I won't tell, I said to myself, *about hiding under the covers, or fear, or fires, or burning lamps—anything. I'll never tell.*

ELEVEN
The Petersons

After Lars had returned with the pail of fresh water, he began to haul wood. He did not stop until I insisted that I would be unable to get out of my house if he brought in any more. He grinned, then proceeded to chop a fine supply of kindling. I wanted to offer him a quarter, but somehow I felt that it wouldn't be right in the eyes of his mother who had sent him over; so, instead, I fixed him a few more slices of bread and jam. He sat on my step and ate them, while I sat beside him.

"How many students do you think I'll have?"

"'Bout eighteen or nineteen, or more maybe if da bigger boys come."

Perhaps twenty students, of all ages and abilities. It seems like an awesome task.

"Ve only haf desks fer sixteen, so da ot'ers vill haf to haf tables an' benches," Lars continued.

"And who will look after getting tables and benches?" I asked him, knowing that he was right about the desks. I had counted them the night before but had seen no evidence of tables or benches.

"Mr. Laverly asked Mr. Yohnson to build 'em. He's a car—car—builder."

I smiled. "I see. Will they be ready for Monday, do you think?"

"S'pose to be."

Lars finished his last bit of bread, "I'd better go. Mama vill need me. T'anks fer da bread and yam. Oh, yah. Ma says, 'come to supper tonight.' Six o'clock. Right over dat vay—cross da field. Can ya come?"

"I'd be delighted."

He frowned slightly, "Does dat mean ya vill?"

"I will."

"Good." And with a grin, he was gone.

"Thank you for the wood and water," I called after him.

I spent the rest of the day sorting through my little house, making a list of the items I would need to purchase and wishing desperately that I had my trunks. Mr. Laverly did not come by as I had hoped, and I had no way of knowing where or how to contact him.

At twenty minutes to six I straightened my hair, brushed off my dress, and set out to find the Petersons. Lars was right. As soon as I passed through the growth of trees behind the school grounds, I could see their farm sitting on the side of the next hill. At times I lost sight of it as I passed through other groves of trees, but my bearings seemed to hold true; it was always there, just where I expected it to be, whenever I emerged from the woods.

Anna Peterson greeted me with a warm smile. Her English was broken, and she spoke with a heavy accent, but her eyes danced with humor as she laughed at her own mistakes.

"Ve are so glad ya come. Ve need school bad—so chil'ren don't talk none like me."

Mr. Peterson "velcomed" me too, and the warmth of their friendliness made it easy for me to respond. Olga and Peter were very shy. Else was a bit more outgoing, though still quick to drop her gaze and step back if I spoke directly to her.

Anna was a good cook. The simple ingredients in her big kitchen produced mouth-watering food. It was awfully nice to enjoy a meal with a family again.

The evening went quickly, and before I knew it, I could see the sun sinking slowly toward the treetops. Dusk was stealing over the land, making me feel like curling up and purring with contentment.

"I must go," I announced. "I hadn't realized—it will soon be dark and I'm not very sure of my way."

"Lars vill go vid. He knows da vay gud."

I accepted Lars' company with gratitude.

Mrs. Peterson insisted on giving me a basket of food—milk, cream, butter, eggs, bread, and fresh vegetables from her garden. I tried to explain that I still had milk and cream on hand.

"T'row out milk. Vill be no gud," she insisted. "Save cream for baking, maybe. Make lots gud t'ings vid sour cream. Ve vill send more t'ings vid Lars to school for 'you."

"I will be happy to buy . . ."

"Buy not'ing. I gif. I glad you here. Now my boys an' girls learn—learn to speak, to read. I don't teach—I don't know. Now dey teach me."

"I'll show you, Mama," Else spoke up. "I'll show you all I learn."

"Yah, little vun teach big vun," Mrs. Peterson smiled, placing a loving hand on Else's head. " 'Tis gud."

Lars and I walked slowly through the twilight. I allowed him, at his insistence, to carry the basket. Already I loved him and his family and could hardly wait for Monday, to meet the other children of the community.

We were about halfway home when a now-familiar but nonetheless heart-stopping howl rent the stillness. My first impulse was to lift my skirts and dash for home, but I restrained myself. I'm sure my face must have lost all of its color, and my hands fluttered to my breast, but Lars didn't seem to notice. He was telling me about his Holstein heifer calf and didn't even break his sentence.

The howl came again and was joined by many others. Lars merely raised his voice to speak above the din. I fought hard to keep from panicking. Eventually Lars probably noticed my reaction and commented, "Silly ole coyotes. Sure make a racket. Sound like yust behind next clump, yet dey vay over in da field."

Then he went on with his story.

Lars' easy dismissal of the animals reassured me, and my heart slowly returned to its normal beat.

When we reached the teacherage, Lars went in with me. He

found the matches and lit the lamp, then unloaded the basket of food onto my small cupboard.

"Ya be needin' a fire?"

"Not tonight. It's plenty warm, and I won't be staying up long."

I was beginning to feel weary from the lack of sleep the night before.

"Guess I go now," said Lars. He walked toward the door, basket in hand.

"Thank you so much, Lars, for seeing me home—and for carrying the basket."

He would never realize the difference that his calm presence had made when the coyotes had begun to howl.

"Yer velcome," he grinned.

"I wish I had some books to send home with you so that you and your sisters might practice reading, but I have none here. All my things are in my trunks, and I need to see Mr. Laverly before I can get them."

"Ya need Mr. Laverly? Vere yer trunks?"

"Still in Lacombe. There wasn't any room to bring them in the automobile."

"Ya need 'em?"

"I certainly do," I said emphatically.

He nodded, then with a wave and grin pushed open the door. " 'Night, Miss T'atcher."

"Good-night, Lars."

I watched him move away in the soft darkness. Soon the moon would rise to give light to the world, but for now his way was still dark—yet he moved forward without uncertainty or fear. The coyotes howled again, but Lars paid no attention to them as he hurried off toward home.

I turned toward the coyotes now. They still made little tingles scurry up and down my spine each time I heard their mournful cry, but I refused to allow panic to seize me.

"Oh, no, you don't," I spoke aloud to them. "You made a

cringing, frightened coward of me last night, but never again—never again!"

Still, I was glad to hook my door behind me as I entered the little teacherage I now called home.

TWELVE

Trip to Town

The next morning before I had even finished my breakfast, a team and wagon turned into my lane. The driver approached my house and knocked on the door, hat in hand. He introduced himself as Mr. Laverly. Lars, my special helper, had already ridden over on horseback to his farm that morning and informed him that I needed my trunks.

"Sorry, ma'am," the man apologized. "Wanted to be over to greet you yesterday right off, but my wagon busted a wheel an' it took nigh all day to fix it. 'Course I had me no idee that you was without yer belongin's, or I'd a borrowed an outfit from a neighbor an' been right over." His round face mirrored his sincere apology.

"I sure feel terrible that yer things didn't get here the same time that you did," he hurried on, wiping his hands and face with a bright square from a pocket. "I was 'opin' to spare ya a trip by wagon over those long, dusty roads. I'd be happy to jest go on in an' pick up yer things fer ya, an' ya can jest wait here."

"Oh, I'd love to go along, Mr. Laverly," I interjected quickly. "The weather is lovely, and the trees are so beautiful—I'm sure that the trip to town will be an enjoyable one in spite of the dust."

He relaxed some—even smiled.

"Would you care for a cup of coffee while I get my hat?" I asked, and he nodded that he would.

I motioned him toward one of the green chairs and poured coffee into the cup with the fewest chips, then cleared the table. When I had things tidied I went to the bedroom.

I did wish that I had another dress. The one that I had been wearing when I arrived hung, dejected and torn, from a peg in my bedroom. I had no sewing supplies with me to repair it. The dress that I now wore was the only other one I had with me. Besides appearing somewhat wrinkled and soiled, it was not the gown that I would have chosen to wear on my first day in a new town and did not go well with my hat.

Looking in some dismay at my reflection in the small cracked mirror, I placed my hat on carefully and pinned it in place. I smoothed out my skirt the best I could and picked up my handbag, then went to inform Mr. Laverly that I was ready when he was. He drained the last of the coffee from the cup and rose to go.

Mr. Laverly was not an eloquent man, I discovered, yet he did tell me of the parents' desire to provide education for the children of Pine Springs. I admired these people for working so hard and long to get someone who would teach, and I felt honored to be that "someone."

At Lacombe, Mr. Laverly dropped me off at the general store and went on to the train station to collect my trunks. I did not dally but set to work filling my long shopping list as quickly as I could. There seemed to be so many things that I needed, but I held myself in check and purchased only essentials—with the exception of one extravagance. I had determined that I would drink my tea like a lady, even in a log house; so I purchased a teapot and two cups and saucers of fine china. I felt somehow Mama's mind would be much more at ease about me if she knew that I was having my tea in the proper fashion. After all, civilization could not be too far away from Pine Springs if I had such amenities!

I had not finished my shopping when Mr. Laverly returned. He kindly assured me that I needn't rush. He suggested that we meet at one o'clock and perhaps I would like to get myself some lunch at the hotel before we started our long journey back. I agreed, and he went off on some business of his own. I finally rounded up all the items that I needed in order to keep house. I then bought a further supply of staple groceries and set out for the hotel.

While waiting for my meal to arrive, I wrote a short letter to my family and also a note to Jon and his family. I assured them that

I would write more later, but I did want them to know that I had arrived safely and was very pleased and excited about my living arrangements and my school. I omitted telling Mama just exactly where my school was. She had sent me west to Jonathan and expected me to stay within the shelter of his protection. I shuddered to think how she would feel if she knew that I was about one hundred and fifty long, slow miles away from him.

My food arrived, and I placed my brief notes in the addressed envelopes. The waitress said I could post them right there at the hotel.

Mr. Laverly, true to his word, appeared at one o'clock. We returned to the store, and he and the clerk loaded my purchases. I looked longingly at the inviting little town, wishing that I had time to explore it, but Mr. Laverly was now in a hurry to be on his way.

The September afternoon sun rode hot and high in the sky. The horses sauntered along, and the wagon bumped and jostled. With each mile, I came to realize more why Mr. Laverly had been concerned about saving me this trip. My excitement and the loveliness of the weather and scenery had gotten me to town without too much discomfort, but I began to feel that the trip home would never end.

By the time we arrived at the teacherage, I was hot, tired, dirty and sore. Nothing would interest me more than a long soak in a hot tub; and then I remembered—I had no such thing, except for the round metal washtub I had just purchased that day for my laundry. Well, it would have to do.

Mr. Laverly unloaded all of my belongings. The trunks were heavy for one person, and I insisted upon giving him a hand. It was a difficult task to get all the things from the wagon into the teacherage, and my help, though freely offered, was barely adequate.

When finally everything was in my house, and Mr. Laverly had graciously refused my offer of a cup of tea, I remembered to ask him about the schoolhouse door. He had the nails out in a jiffy, and then his wagon rumbled out of the yard.

Gone were the thoughts of a bath in my excitement at getting settled. With a feverish eagerness I attacked the trunks and the purchases and began to make myself a home in the "wilderness." Dusk was approaching and I still had not stopped for breath. I was weary, dusty, and hungry, and if I didn't stop, I would be exhausted. Though tired, I gazed around me with pleasure. It did look and feel much more like home now, but darkness would come soon and if I wanted a bath, I needed to haul the water for it.

I placed my new boiler on the stove and poured the water from the pail into it. Then I ran for more water, pumping in near panic. If the coyotes were to begin their howling right now, I wasn't sure that I, as yet, would be strong enough to face them alone. Fortunately, I was just entering the house with my second pail of water when the first howl broke over me. *I really don't need more water anyway,* I assured myself and fastened the door behind me.

I started the fire in the stove beneath the boiler and also made room on the stove top to put on the kettle for tea. I fixed a simple meal, which I practically wolfed down in my hunger, and then I drank my tea slowly from my new teacup, staring at the other teacup as I drank. Would there ever be a second person in my little teacherage to share my teatime? Suddenly a wave of loneliness overtook me. I was happy here, but I was alone. I longed for Julie, and then realized that even she would not properly fill the void I was feeling. Julie would be bubbly and chatty and light. I needed someone with serenity, strength, purposefulness to share my thoughts and my days. Someone like—and my mind involuntarily began to review the men that I had known. Each face that appeared in my mind's eye was readily dismissed. Then suddenly, without warning, I saw again the face of Jon's friend. The intense eyes, the slight smile, and the strength of character that was evident was attractive and yet made me stir uneasily. In spite of the fact that not another soul was anywhere near, I found myself blushing in embarrassment at my foolishness. Changing my thoughts to safer things, I stood quickly, teacup in hand, and proceeded to add wood to the fire. Oh, how I was anticipating that hot bath!

While I waited for the water to heat, I carried my small washtub to my bedroom and placed it on the rug. Then I began the slow procedure of dipping and transporting the warm water to fill it. By the time I had finally finished my preparations, the water had cooled considerably. *Next time,* I informed myself, *I must begin with the water on the hot side.*

I stepped into the small tub and experimented with ways to curl myself into it. *Why didn't I buy the larger one?* I chided myself. I twisted and turned and curled and uncurled, but there was no way that I could get all of me into the tub at one time. Finally I hung my legs out over the edge in hopes of getting the warm water onto the aching parts of my body. It wasn't very satisfactory. Still sore from the wagon's jostling, I finally gave up the effort. Drying myself thoroughly, I slipped into my warmest nightgown and snuggled under the quilts. I would empty the tub of water in the morning.

Safe in bed, I listened to an occasional coyote howl. It didn't sound so spine-chilling now. In fact, I imagined that, with a little time, a person might even be able to get used to it.

THIRTEEN

Saturday

When I awoke the next morning, I felt stiff all over. I was tempted to stay under the covers, but my body would not allow me the privilege. I thought of the small structure marked "Girls" way across the clearing and wondered if my legs would be able to walk the distance. I did wish that they had thought to build it nearer the teacherage.

I dressed clumsily and started walking slowly. The sun was up and shining down on a picture-pretty world. By the time I had traveled across to the building and back, some of the kinks were loosening, and I decided that I would be able to face the day after all, even emptying the tub of cold bath water!

While I waited for the water to heat for my morning coffee, I took my Bible and turned to the passage in Nehemiah where I had been reading. Though Nehemiah was leading a whole nation and rebuilding a city, I found some exciting parallels between his story and my new life way out here in the Canadian frontier. The day suddenly seemed to hold great promise. The kettle was singing merrily before I finished my prayer, and I proceeded to fix my breakfast.

I spent the morning carrying books and classroom aids to the little schoolhouse, then made a quick lunch and spent the afternoon organizing things. The classroom soon looked inhabited and inviting. I even wrote a few simple adding exercises on the blackboard. I hung the alphabet and number charts, put up some study pictures and maps, and the room began to come alive.

Around five o'clock while I was still lingering in the classroom, choosing the Psalms that I would read for the opening on Monday morning, I heard the jingle of harness. It was Mr. Johnson delivering the tables and benches. He had a near-grown son with him who took one look at me and went red to the very roots of his hair. I pretended not to notice, to save him further embarrassment, and showed them where to place the furniture. Mr. Johnson gazed around the now-furnished classroom, and tears began to gather in his eyes and trickle down his creased cheeks.

"Da Lord be praised!" he exclaimed. "It really be so. Ve do haf school. Yah?"

His deep feelings touched me.

After they had gone, I surveyed the schoolroom again, my feelings swinging between pride and apprehension. Walking back and forth, touching each article, changing this or that, rearranging something here or there, I was only too aware that I had very few aids to assist me in teaching these children. How I wished that I had more—but that was foolishness. I would just have to do what I could with what I had.

After writing "My name is Miss Thatcher" in block letters on the blackboard, I reluctantly turned to go home to prepare my evening meal.

Monday, I thought, *please come quickly—lest I burst.*

As I walked toward the door, I noticed a printed list posted beside it. I had not spotted it before, and I now stopped to read it. It was captioned, "Rules for the Teacher," and my eyes ran quickly down the page. They read as follows:

1. A teacher may not marry during the school year.
2. Lady teachers are not to keep company with men.
3. Lady teachers must be home between the hours of 8:00 P.M. and 6:00 A.M., unless attending a school function.
4. Man teachers must not chew tobacco.
5. There must be no loitering, by male or female, in downtown stores or ice-cream parlors.
6. A teacher may not travel outside the district limits without permission from the school-board chairman.
7. Neither male nor female may smoke.
8. Bright colors are not to be worn, either in or out of school.

9. Under no circumstances may a lady teacher dye her hair.
10. A lady teacher must wear at least two petticoats.
11. Dresses must not be shorter than touching the ankle.
12. To keep the schoolroom neat and tidy, the teacher must sweep the floor and clean the chalkboard every day.
13. The schoolroom floor must be scrubbed with hot, soapy water at least once a week.
14. The teacher must start the fire, when needed, by 8:00 A.M. so that the room will be warm for the pupils by 9:00 A.M.

I didn't expect to have any trouble obeying the lengthy list; still, it bothered me some to be dictated to in such a fashion. At first I was going to blame the whole thing on Mr. Higgins; but then I remembered other such lists that I had read and realized this one wasn't so different after all. I decided to pretend that I hadn't seen it. I would have observed all of its mandates anyway.

FOURTEEN

Sunday

There wasn't any reason for my early rising on Sunday except perhaps habit. After I had carefully dressed and groomed my hair, I fussed about my small kitchen, fixing myself a *special* breakfast, as had been our tradition at home on Sunday mornings. It really didn't turn out to be very special, for I had gained very little experience in cooking. I determined that I would put time and effort into learning how to prepare tasty dishes. *No matter one's education or other abilities, a woman should be able to hold her head up proudly in her own kitchen,* I decided.

After I had cleared away the mess I had managed to make, I went outside for a walk. The sunshine felt good on my shoulders and back where the stiffness from my wagon ride still made me feel old and creaky. I wanted to lie down in the grass and let the warm rays do for me what my inadequate tub had not been able to do.

The morning hours seemed to lag. Eventually I returned to the house, hoping that my clock would tell me it was now time for me to prepare my noon meal. It was still plenty early, but I started the preparations anyway.

Again I ate, cleared away and cleaned up, all without using up very many minutes out of the lengthy day.

In the afternoon I read more about Nehemiah and spent time in prayer. I missed, more than I had ever thought possible, our church back home. I thought, too, of Jon and Mary and the family in Calgary and the Sundays that I had enjoyed worshiping with them in their small church. I should have thought to ask the Petersons if there was a church nearby where I might meet on Sundays with other believers. I couldn't imagine living, Sunday after Sunday, without an opportunity for worship and fellowship. How dry the endless days would become with no Sunday service to revive and refresh one's spirit!

I was sorely tempted to find some excuse to journey over to the Petersons, but my Eastern reserve and mother-taught manners held me in check. I had not been invited; one did not impose upon others.

I tried to read; I took short, unsatisfactory walks; I fixed afternoon tea; and all the time I ached with loneliness, and the day dragged on.

About six-thirty I heard voices. It was Lars and Else. I don't recall ever being happier about seeing visitors. I fairly ran to meet them! They must have seen my eagerness, but Else held back as Lars walked with me to my door.

"Lars," she whispered, " 'member."

"Yah," he answered, but kept on walking.

"But Mama said," Else persisted.

"It's okay," Lars said, seeming a little exasperated.

"What is it?" I asked.

"Mama said not to bot'er you."

"She said, 'if Miss T'atcher vas busy or didn't vant company,' " Lars informed Else. "She's not busy." He turned to me quickly, "Are ya?"

"Oh, no." I hurried to assure them, lest they get away from me. "And I'd really like some company."

I sat down on my step, and they joined me. It had been such a lonely day.

"I'm not used to a Sunday all alone, nor am I used to a Sunday without going to church. Is there any church around here?"

"Nope—not yet," said Lars. "Mama vould sure like vun, but dere are only two Lut'ran families—not 'nough fer a church."

"Ve have church," Else corrected her brother in great astonishment.

"Not *in* a church," Lars replied.

"Still, church," she insisted.

"Where?" I asked, excited about any kind of service.

"In the school," Else said.

I was confused.

"But I've been here all day—no one came."

"I know," Lars said. "Mr. Laverly said dat ve vouldn't haf it today. He said dat da new teacher might not be happy wid us all meetin' here, messin' up t'ings. Ve'd yust haf to vait an' see."

"So that's it," I said, thankful that I wouldn't have to put in another Sunday like this one. "I will speak to Mr. Laverly, and we'll have church as usual next Sunday."

Else's eyes lit up, and I could tell that she, too, had missed church that day. Lars didn't appear to care too much one way or the other.

"Ma says, 'Ya need anyt'ing?' "

"No—no—nothing. You hauled such a good wood supply that I still have plenty. The days are nice and warm, and I let the fire go out as soon as I have finished cooking my food."

"An' vater?"

"It's good for me to haul my own water. I just finished getting a bucket."

I glanced down at my hands. My scratches were healing nicely, but already my hands had lost their well-cared-for look. I wasn't unduly upset by it, but I wasn't especially pleased with the new look either. Julie would laugh, or cry out in alarm, if she could see my hands now. I smiled.

Looking back at Lars, I suddenly thought of Matthew. How good it would be to have him here with me! For some reason, which I couldn't put my finger on, I decided that this land would be good for my young brother Matthew also.

Else's quiet question brought my mind back to my visitors.

"Did ya get da books?" she asked in a soft voice.

"Yes—yes, I did. Mr. Laverly came right over after you saw him on Friday, Lars. I must thank you for going over so promptly."

Lars flushed slightly at my thanks, so I hurried on. "We went to Lacombe in the wagon and got all of my things. I've unpacked everything and organized both the schoolroom and my house. Do you want to see them?"

I could tell by Else's eyes that she did, so I led the way.

The house was certainly nothing fancy. I had brought very little with me in the way of furnishings—a few pictures of my family, a spread for my bed, a soft rug, a few favorite ornaments, some dresser scarves and small pillows; but they managed to give my little home a feeling of warmth. It was plain to see that Else was impressed. Even Lars seemed to notice the difference.

"It's nice," he said.

I saw Else's eyes skim over everything, then rest on my china teapot and cups and saucers. I knew at once who would be the first person that I would invite for a cup of tea—though she was but six years old. She could drink milk from the cup if she preferred.

Even as Else's eyes assured me that she appreciated my little house, they also declared that something was missing. At length she gave voice to her concern.

"Is dat all da books?" She pointed at my Bible and the book of poetry with which I had attempted to fill my day.

"Oh, no. I have no bookshelves you see, so I had to leave my books in the trunk."

I raised the lid of one of my trunks to show her the volumes that had become my good friends over the years. Her eyes caressed them.

"Maybe you'd like to see the school. I took the books for classroom use over there."

They both flashed excited glances at each other, so together we walked to the school.

If I had been in doubt about teaching in a one-room classroom with students who had never had any formal learning, I would have lost all such doubts after seeing their response to their first look at the school.

First they stopped and stared, their eyes traveling over everything. Lars began to softly name the letters on the alphabet chart, while Else migrated toward the meager stacks of primers and books on the two small shelves at the front of the room. I went with her and lifted a book from the others.

"Here, try this one," I encouraged her. "You may look at the pictures if you'd like."

She took the book, crossed to a desk, and sat down. She gently turned each page, missing nothing as her eyes eagerly drank in the pictures and her mind sought for the words on the printed pages.

Time passed quickly. Before we had realized it, the sun was crawling into bed. Lars, who had also chosen a book and retreated to a desk, looked up in unbelief.

"Ve gotta go," he said quickly. "Mama vill vorry. Come, Else."

Reluctantly Else handed me the book.

"Why don't you take it home with you and show it to Olga and Peter? I'm sure that they would like to see it, too. You may bring it back in the morning."

She hesitated, wondering if she was worthy of being entrusted with such a treasure.

"Go ahead," I said. "Lars may take his, too."

They ran off then, now eager to get home for more than one reason. I walked slowly back to the teacherage.

I felt contented now. I was sure that in the evening hours I would be able to enjoy Wordsworth, Longfellow, or Keats. Perhaps my heart wouldn't even skip a beat tonight at the howling of the coyotes. I sat warm and comfortable in my lumpy chair and sipped tea from my china cup. I knew that tomorrow held great promise.

FIFTEEN

School Begins

I was up with the birds on Monday morning. I was far too excited to sleep. I had always enjoyed teaching, but never before had it affected me in quite this way; the eagerness of the people in the area had rubbed off on me.

The bell was to be rung at nine o'clock. I felt that I had already lived two full days that morning before nine o'clock arrived.

Dressing carefully, I did my hair in the most becoming way that I knew. It really was too fussy for the classroom, but I couldn't reason myself out of it. I tried to eat my breakfast but didn't feel at all hungry, so I finally gave up and cleaned up my kitchen area.

I left early for the classroom and dusted and polished, rearranged and prepared, and still the hands on the clock had hardly moved.

The first students arrived at twenty to nine. Cindy and Sally Blake were accompanied by their mother and father. Mr. Blake was a quiet man—but every family can use *one* quiet member, I decided. Mrs. Blake was chattering before she even climbed down from the wagon, and didn't actually cease until the schoolroom door closed upon her departing figure.

The Clarks came together—seven of them. It took me a few moments to sort them all out, and the harder I tried the more confused I became. It helped when I learned that there were two families involved, cousins—three from one family and four from the other.

Mrs. Dickerson brought her small son in by the hand. I think she had hoped he would be shy and reluctant to leave her side, but his face brightened at the first glimpse of his school.

Others came too quickly for me to learn each name as they entered. I would have to wait until the bell rang and the students had taken their places—and their parents had returned home.

I smiled at the Peterson children. Else and Lars presented me with carefully wrapped packages. Their mother wanted the precious books to be returned safely without soil, so she had wrapped them in brown paper and tied them securely with string.

The morning was spent in organizing a roll call and trying to determine the grade level of each student. Even the older ones had previously had very little opportunity to learn, so it was going to be "back to basics" for the first few weeks of my teaching. I prayed that I would be able to present the simple lessons in a manner that would not offend the older students. It was difficult to include a girl of fourteen with a row of six-year-olds for a lesson on the alphabet or the phonic sounds without making her feel embarrassed, but I'd need to devise a way to do it.

Not all of the students were eager to attend school. I picked out three who, for one reason or another, seemed to prefer going their own way on this lovely fall morning.

Sally Clark seemed rather absent-minded and uncaring. She was fifteen and probably reasoned that if she had managed thus far without school, why bother now? Besides, she would likely marry in a few years, and she could already bake bread, make quilts, and care for babies. Time spent in a classroom with a lot of little children seemed like a total waste of time.

Eight-year-old Andy Pastachuck may have wanted to learn, but it was clear that he wasn't capable of learning very much. I was told that Andy had been kicked by a horse when he was three years old. The side of his head bore a rugged, vicious scar, and I concluded that Andy's little mind bore a scar as well. I determined that I would do all that I could for him. With his older sister, Teresa, I longed to find some way to protect him from the cruel, angry world.

David Dickerson had no problem with ability. He was wiry, witty, and had a constant, seemingly uncontrollable energy. He wished to be at all places and involved in all things at once and found it most difficult to sit still long enough for a *fact* to catch up to him. This six-year-old thrived on ideas rather than information and jumped quickly from one to another. *If I can ever corral all that energy and steer it in the right direction,* I thought, *I'll have an exceptionally capable student.* In the meantime, David seemed to wish to be in the wheatfield, the playground, on his pony, up a pine tree—anywhere but quietly seated at a desk in the classroom. Still, he did have a hunger for knowledge, and I was sure that if I could only get him to sit still long enough, he would learn quickly.

By the end of our first day spent together, I had been able to introduce my pupils to the open door of learning; but I knew that many difficult days lay ahead before I would be able to sort them into legitimate classes. Certainly I couldn't divide them by age. I would have to wait and discover their learning abilities.

I went home from my first day in the classroom excited and exhausted. Every student I had—and there were nineteen—needed individual tutoring. Would I be able to handle it? Where would the time come from? How long before some of them could work on their own?

It seemed that my only recourse was to prepare individual assignments, both after school at night and before school each morning. Then each member of the class would have something to work on as I took time with the individual lessons.

I sighed deeply at the awesome task that lay ahead of me. Reminding myself that it was a challenge but not an impossibility, I squared my shoulders as I entered the teacherage door.

I brewed some tea and carried the teapot and my china cup to my chair and sat down. Poking at some of the chair stuffing to make it fit me better, I decided I should get some sort of footstool so that I could put my feet up for a few minutes at the end of the day. I recalled seeing a small wooden crate in the storage shed. Surely I could find enough pieces of material in my sewing basket to cover it. I planned that it would be my next Saturday's project.

As I relaxed in my big chair and sipped the hot tea, I thought about each student and how best I could teach him. As soon as I had drained my cup, I began preparing some simple assignments. I worked well into the late evening by the wavering light of the lamp. Tonight even the howling of the coyotes failed to distract me.

The week was a busy one. I arose early each morning to write assignments on the blackboard and to add last-minute ideas to the lessons that I had prepared on paper. The day was given entirely to the students. Already some of them were beginning to show abilities in one area or another. A small group was slowly emerging who would be able to take a forward step in arithmetic. Another group was ready to go on in the second primer. Two students showed real promise in art and three had musical ability.

Daily I felt frustrated by my lack of materials for teaching. *If only I had . . .* I often started thinking. But I didn't have, so I tried to make up for the lack with creativity.

At the end of the classroom time, I lingered for a few moments to correct work and plan the next day, then rushed home, made my cup of tea, and rested for a few moments in my overstuffed chair. All the time that I sipped, my mind refused to relax. It leaped from one idea to another, from plan to plan. As soon as my cup was empty I returned to work in the classroom, trying to put my ideas to work.

By the end of the week I was physically weary, but I was perhaps the happiest I had ever been in my life. I had planned to work on the footstool on Saturday, but instead I asked my students if they knew of anyone with whom I could ride into town, The growing list of items that I might find to assist me in the classroom prompted this request. I dreaded another long trip to town in a bumpy wagon, but I couldn't very well hand the list over to someone else and expect him to do the shopping for me.

To my delight, Sally Clark brought word on Friday that her folks were going to town on Saturday and would be happy to pick me up at eight o'clock the next morning.

SIXTEEN

Joint Tenants

True to their word, the Clarks arrived at ten to eight. My list and I were ready to go. I did not plan to make a weekly trip to Lacombe, so I had tried to think of all that I might be needing in the near future.

One of the needs came to my attention when I discovered that I was not living alone. How many other occupants the house held was still unknown to me, but it was easy to tell by the evidence that I found on several mornings that I was sharing my home with a family of mice.

I guess the mice felt that *I* was the intruder; it was apparent that they assumed the entire place belonged to them.

The first morning that I saw the evidence, I was frightened. I had never lived with mice before. What if they were to climb into my bed and nibble my fingers or, horrors of horrors, become tangled in my hair? What could I do about them? How did one go about getting rid of mice? I added mousetraps to my list, but I wasn't sure what I was to look for. I had never seen a mousetrap.

The next morning I had found a corner nibbled from my fresh loaf of bread. Now I was angry—the nerve of the little beasts! There was no way that I was going to share my home *and* my food with rodents. I boldly underlined mousetraps on my list.

Before I went to bed the next night, I placed all my foodstuffs in the cupboards, out of the rodents' reach. On the fourth morning of my busy teaching week, I found evidence of the mice having romped over my dishes—right in my cupboards! I was furious and repelled. I took all of the dishes from my cupboards, washed them in hot, soapy water and scalded them with boiling water from the teakettle, all the while breathing vengeance against those nasty creatures. Indeed, something had to be done. I thought of sending a note to Mr. Laverly with one of the students who passed by his farm, but I stubbornly rejected the idea. Surely I could handle a little problem like mice.

So, as I traveled to town on that overcast Saturday morning, sitting on a makeshift seat in the Clarks' wagon, I thought about my unwelcome tenants. After today I would be rid of them, for I planned to leave traps throughout the house. I felt no pity whatever for the creatures who would be caught in those traps.

As soon as the Clarks dropped me off at the general store, I set to work on my list. I could find only a portion of the items that I had desired for the classroom. In a few instances I made substitutions. In many cases I was forced to do without.

I purchased a large washtub—the biggest I could find, determined that I would have a decent soak when I took my bath.

I carefully selected all of the food items that I felt I needed and added a few metal containers to store them in. No more would mice be sharing my loaf of bread while I waited for my traps to do their job.

"Now," I said to the long-nosed clerk, "I need mousetraps—the best that you have."

I don't know what I expected him to show me, but certainly not that little bit of wood and wire.

"This is a mousetrap?"

"Yes, ma'am."

"Is that all you have?"

"What did you have in mind, ma'am?"

"Well—I'm—I'm not sure. I've never needed—but I thought . . . How does that catch them—what holds them in? There's no cage."

"No, ma'am." I think that he smiled, though he turned too quickly for me to be sure.

"Why don't they run off?" I persisted.

"They don't run off, ma'am—'cause they're *dead,*" he answered me, his face solemn but his eyes twinkling.

"Dead?"

"Yes, ma'am."

"What kills them?"

"The trap, ma'am."

I looked at the small thing, bewildered.

He finally picked up a trap and, as though speaking to a small child, proceeded to show me.

"You place the bait here, ma'am—just a touch. Then you pull this back and hook it, gently, like this. You place it carefully in the path you think the mouse will follow. He comes to steal the bait"—he reached out with the pencil from behind his ear—"and—."

There was a sharp bang, and the trap sprang forward—and I backward. The pencil was snapped in the firm grip of the trap. I staggered over bails of twine that were stacked behind me on the floor and nearly lost my balance while color flooded my cheeks. The clerk bent his head down as he freed his pencil from the trap—and, I imagine, composed his face.

"I'll take ten of them," I said with all of the dignity that I could muster.

"Ten?" He cleared his throat and blinked. "So many?"

"I have no idea how many mice there are."

"One trap is usable over and over, ma'am."

This was further news to me.

"You just lift the wire," the clerk explained patiently, "release the dead mouse and reset."

It sounded easy enough.

"Fine," I said. "I'll take one."

He put the trap with my other purchases.

By the time the Clarks returned to pick me up, I and my new belongings were ready for the long trip home.

There was still daylight left when we arrived home, so I started to work on the footstool. Rather than piecing material from the bits and scraps in my sewing basket, I had decided to purchase some sturdy material in town. I had even bought some batting so that the footstool would be padded.

Humming as I sewed and tacked, I found this project challenging and gratifying. I was pleased with my first attempt as furnituremaker. I even had enough material left to make a small pillow to match the stool.

By the time I had sorted my purchases, placing those in the schoolroom that belonged there and the others in my house, it was late and I was weary.

I dragged my large tub into my bedroom, poured the water that I had heated and enjoyed my bath. It wasn't like our fine tub at home, but I could at least sit in it and splash the water over the rest of me.

It had been a good week, I decided, as I crawled into bed. I felt that I had made progress in the classroom. The children were learning. I had a tub big enough for bathing, and I—I hadn't set the mousetrap! I climbed out of my warm bed and re-lit the lamp, burning my fingers on the still-hot chimney.

It looked so easy when the man in the store had demonstrated it. It wasn't easy at all. I rubbed a small portion of butter on the metal bait piece, and then stretched the wire back—back. I was trying to fasten it down when—"ping"—it snapped together and flew from my hand across the floor. Shaken, I went after it, feeling as if it were capable of attacking me. Again I tried and again it snapped. The sixth attempt got my finger, and I cried out in anger and frustration. I wasn't sure what I was the most angry at—the homesteading mice or the offensive trap.

Finally, on about the tenth try, I managed to secure the wire, and I gingerly placed the unruly bit of wood and metal on the floor by the cupboard. Eyeing its location, I decided to move it over just a bit with my foot when—"ping"—it sprang into the air. I jumped and struck my hip against the stove.

Almost in tears, I again went through the procedure. Eventually the trap was set and placed on the ideal spot. As I inspected it now, I couldn't see any butter left on the little projection intended for the bait, but I refused to touch the thing again.

I blew out the lamp and crawled back into bed. My finger was still smarting and my hip throbbed from its encounter with the hard iron of the stove. I snuggled under the warm quilt and tried to think of things more pleasant than mousetraps and unwelcome guests.

I suppose that it was about one o'clock when the sharp "ping" of the trap brought me upright in my bed, staring toward the open door of my bedroom. In my drowsy state, I did not understand where the sound had come from, but I then remembered what had taken so much of my time the night before. Well, at least it had worked. Maybe now my problems with unwanted roommates would be over.

I snuggled back down but I couldn't go to sleep. The thought of an animal out there in my kitchen, all tangled up in the metal of that trap, disturbed me. What should I do about it? Should I go and release it at once? Was it already too late? But I couldn't bring myself to face the situation by the flickering light of my lamp.

The dawn was approaching when I finally was able to doze off.

When I awakened again it was full daylight. At first I felt alarmed, realizing that I had slept long past my usual waking hour. Then I remembered it was Sunday and settled back to enjoy the comfort of my bed for a few more minutes. I planned a leisurely day, thankful indeed that today there would be a church service in the schoolroom. I had sent the message home with all of the pupils that I would be only too happy to share the community school with a Sunday congregation, and the service had been set for two o'clock.

I wasn't used to an afternoon service, and it seemed a long time to wait, but at least it was something to look forward to. Surely I would be able to somehow fill the long morning hours with productive activities while I waited. I began to take a mental inventory of what I had on hand to read.

I crawled out of bed, stretching and flexing my muscles. If I didn't lie just right on my mattress, I could wake up with some stubborn kinks. This morning I seemed to have several. I wasn't concerned. I had all morning to gradually work them out.

I slipped on my robe and slippers and headed for my stove. I'd make the fire and start the coffee.

In my early morning reverie, I very nearly failed to notice a small object on my floor. I was just about to lower my right foot on it when I jerked back with a gasp. My mousetrap had jumped halfway across the floor from its original position. There it lay, and securely clamped to the wood base was a limp, dead mouse.

I shall not describe further the sight that met my eyes or my revulsion as I looked at it. My first thought was to run, but I soon stifled my panic and convinced myself that the trap and its victim could do me very little bodily harm.

My next thought was not a welcome one—it was up to *me* to care for the furry corpse in my pathway. Somehow I must remove the mouse from the trap if I were to have the trap for future use, as the clerk in the store had indicated. The thought of touching it made me shudder. I couldn't. I knew I couldn't. At length I took the broom and dustpan and swept the whole thing up. Holding the dustpan at arm's length, I marched outside and across the clearing. The helpful clerk had said to simply release the dead mouse and reset the trap. How clever—and how impossible.

I walked resolutely on, trying to keep my eyes from the contents of the dustpan. I neared the two small buildings at the far side of the clearing. Glancing furtively about to make sure that no one was watching, I headed for the one marked "Boys." I did not want to share even my outhouse with the dead mouse.

As quickly as I could, I stepped into the building and dumped the mouse, trap and all, down the hole. I then hurried out, again glancing about as one committing a crime, and headed back to the house.

I took a scrub pail and washed the floor where the mouse had lain, my dustpan, and even my broom; and then I began to scrub my hands. I never did succeed that morning in making them feel really clean, so I didn't bother fixing any breakfast. Instead, I poured a cup of coffee (I didn't have to actually touch that), picked up my Bible, and headed for the classroom. I would calm myself, read and pray, and wait for the afternoon service.

SEVENTEEN
Sunday Service

Not too many had arrived at the school by two o'clock. The Petersons were the first to appear. Because the day was cloudy and cool, Lars was allowed to build a fire in the big stove.

The Dickersons came and then the Blakes, the Johnsons and a family by the name of Thebeau. They had two teenage sons who would not be in school until after the harvest—if at all.

Mr. Dickerson was in charge of the service. We sang several songs and read scripture. Mrs. Thebeau gave a Bible lesson for the children, then Mr. Dickerson gave some thoughts on a passage of scripture. It was *not* a sermon, he clarified, because he was *not* a preacher. He voiced some worthwhile insights, and I appreciated his direct approach. I even found myself thinking that it was a shame he was *not* a preacher.

As we stood around visiting after the short service, other teams began pulling into the schoolyard. My first thought was that they had misunderstood the time for the afternoon meeting and were arriving late. What a shame!

I glanced about me. To my surprise there was activity going on all around me in the schoolroom. The fire had been built up and a large kettle of water placed on to heat. Tables were being pushed together, items laid out upon them, and men were busy rearranging the desks. Seeing my puzzled look, Anna Peterson crossed over to me.

"Da folks wanta meet da new teacher. Dis be gud vay, yah?"

I was astounded. But as the afternoon went on I agreed with Anna. Yes, this was a good way. All of my students and their parents were there—except for Phillip Delaney and his parents; they, I was informed, were very sorry to miss the gathering but they were, of necessity, in Calgary for the weekend. Others from the community, though they did not have children of school age, took advantage of the opportunity to get together with the neighbors and perhaps to satisfy curiosity about the new schoolmarm. They all welcomed me heartily.

There were a few men whom I presumed to be unmarried. Two of them were in their twenties, I would have guessed, and the others were older. Three of them in particular made me uncomfortable—I wasn't used to such open stares. One was especially bold. I was afraid that he might approach me, but he never left his companions. I hoped that I wouldn't be thrown into his company at some future date.

Unconsciously, I found myself watching for a possible glimpse of Wynn, but I did not see him. It was obvious that he was not concerned about meeting the new schoolteacher. A foolish disappointment trailed me about the room as I made the acquaintance of my new neighbors. I forced the ridiculous thought from my mind.

I liked my new neighbors. In comparison to my upbringing, they lacked refinement and polish; but they were open and friendly, and I respected their spirit of venture and their sense of humor. They were hearty people, these pioneers. They knew how to laugh and, obviously, they knew how to work.

When the last of the group had returned to their homes, I walked slowly to my teacherage, my heart singing. I already felt that I was a part of this community, and I liked the feeling. I was completely happy here; then I thought of my still-present mice companions, and my song left me. What would I do with them? Live with them, I guessed. . . .

EIGHTEEN

Letters

I was busy chalking an assignment on the blackboard the following afternoon when I heard a firm rap. Before I could respond, the door began to open, so I continued on with my writing, thinking that it was a student who had forgotten some item.

"Be right with you," I said without turning around, and set out to finish the sentence that I was writing.

"That's fine, Miss Thatcher," came a very grown-up, male voice. I swung around leaving a "g" with a very odd, long tail. I'm sure my face must have betrayed my surprise. There was Jon's Calgary friend, Wynn. My breath caught in a gasp and I stood staring for what seemed like eons. My voice would not cooperate in saying the greeting I knew I should extend.

"I'm sorry if I startled you," he began.

"Oh, no—it's fine. It's just—I thought—"

"I've frightened you." His voice held apology.

I shook my head and tried to laugh. It sounded ridiculous, high-pitched and nervous. I decided not to laugh any further.

"I was expecting a student to be standing . . ." My voice sounded nervous also.

"I might have a lot to learn." He smiled and his eyes hinted at teasing. "But I'm afraid that I would look a little out of place in your classroom."

I swallowed, then rubbed at the chalk dust on my hands.

"I'm afraid that I had to miss your party, Miss Thatcher. I hear that it was a success."

"Yes—yes, it was—very nice," I said lamely.

His eyes took in my white-dusted hands that were rubbing

together nervously, then lifted to meet my eyes. Afraid that he was about to make some silly statement about my students being lucky to have such an attractive teacher, I squared my shoulders. He didn't. His eyes shifted to the assignment on the board and then glanced around the room. He stepped away from me and went on a brief tour, carefully taking in all that there was to see. I stood watching him, noticing that even in this small room, he moved with confidence and purpose. Keenly aware of the chalk dust on my frock and the strands of hair that had loosened themselves and wisped about my face, my thoughts tumbled over each other. *What a sight I must be. I probably even have a shiny nose.*

He finished his tour, seeming to approve of what he found.

"I'm so glad that we finally have a school," he said with sincerity, his voice deep and convincing.

"Yes," I almost whispered, "I'm glad too. They are so eager . . ."

Love for my pupils and his unsettling presence made my voice waver, and I was forced to turn from my visitor. I slowly erased the last "g" I had put on the board and rewrote it properly. Finishing the sentence carefully, I put away the chalk I was holding and wiped my hands on a cloth that I kept for the purpose.

"Now, Mr.—Mr.—?" I faltered.

"Forgive me," he said. "I was so fascinated with your room I forgot to introduce myself. I'm Wynn Delaney—longtime friend of your brother Jonathan."

I did not bother to explain that I was quite aware of that last fact.

"How do you do, Mr. Delaney?" I even managed to smile slightly. I admired myself for my control—now that I felt it slowly returning.

"Won't you sit down, Mr. Delaney?"

"Thank you, but no. I must go. I apologize for bursting in on you unannounced and unknown, but I admit to having a feeling of already knowing you. As I said, I've known Jon and Mary for a number of years, and I have seen you—though I was not granted an introduction."

And, I mentally supplied for him, *"I never forget a pretty face"— right, Mr. Delaney.?*

He did not say that, nor anything like it, however. He continued, "I spent the weekend in Calgary and was asked to deliver to you this packet of letters. Mary seemed to feel that it was quite urgent that you receive them to stave off your great loneliness." His eyes twinkled again. "They asked how you were, but I had to confess that I knew nothing, except that school was in session."

He smiled and handed me a bulging envelope.

"Thank you. It was kind of you to act as messengerboy." I hoped that he recognized and appreciated my attempt at humor.

"No problem—since I was going right by. Should I see your family again soon, may I relay that you look to be in good health and spirits?"

"By all means, Mr. Delaney. I am quite enjoying the community and my school."

He nodded his own dismissal with a slight smile, replaced the hat he carried in his hand, and left the schoolroom.

I stood and gazed toward the closed door. I could hear the jingle of harness and the creaking of wheels in the yard, but I did not allow myself the privilege of running to a window.

He had not said that he hoped to see me again. He had not made any mention of finding another excuse to call. He had not even offered any of the light flattery that I was rather accustomed to expect.

A long sigh escaped me, and I turned back to my chalkboard. It was no use. I couldn't concentrate on what I had been doing. I looked down at my hand that held the packet of letters. The letters! Of course, it was the letters from Jon and the family that had disrupted my thoughts. I would hurry home, have my tea, and read my letters. After that I would be myself again and able to gather my thoughts back to my lesson preparation.

I hurried home, built my fire, and put on the kettle. I immediately began digging into my parcel of mail. There was a short note from William telling me about his new schoolteacher, and a copied, carefully penned note from Sarah—my name filled most of one sheet. She also wrote I MISS YOU in big block letters and squeezed her name in at the bottom. There was a sheet with hugs and kisses from Kathleen, and in one corner was a little hug and kiss marked from Elizabeth; Mary had written an explanation that Kathleen insisted Baby Elizabeth have opportunity to send her love as well.

Jon's letter was brief and brotherly, expressing concern for my well-being and happiness, and imploring me to come to Calgary whenever I had opportunity. Mary's letter, a lengthy epistle, included a recitation of everything that had happened in the brief time I had been gone. She added anecdotes and cute sayings from the children. I devoured it all hungrily. I was so glad to hear from them. I wished they were nearer so that I might more readily share my happiness with them.

My tea water had boiled and then cooled because I had neglected to fuel the fire beneath it. I coaxed a flame back to life and nourished it with more kindling and then larger pieces. While the fire took hold again and began to reheat the kettle, I prepared some bread and cheese.

As I sipped my tea and nibbled the bread, my feet resting on my new footstool (which wasn't very ladylike, according to Mother), I again scanned through my letters. I laughed at Mary's comments concerning Mr. Higgins. She had met him at a downtown store, and he had awkwardly asked about me. Mary had replied that she assumed I was just fine, although she had not heard from me since just after I had arrived. He had replied with astonishment, "You mean she stayed?" "Of course she stayed," Mary said. "Isn't that what she was supposed to do?" "Oh, yes—yes, of course," Higgins mumbled and walked off with a red face.

My thoughts kept turning from the letters to their courier, but I refused to let my mind dwell on him. Even though I deliberately tried to keep my mind from straying to Wynn Delaney, I found that the name and the face kept taunting my fancies. Finally I laid aside my teacup, changed my dress, and went out to split wood for my fire. Perhaps some vigorous activity would settle my imagination, I reasoned, and I attacked my woodpile with a vengeance.

NINETEEN

The Living Mousetrap

The following morning I got up to find that the furry squatters had been prancing around on my cupboard top. I *had* to do something! There simply was no living with them. I could not bear sharing my cozy home with the mice.

I again washed and boiled all of my dishes and scrubbed and rubbed everything that I imagined they might have touched. With a great deal of difficulty, I moved two empty metal trunks from my bedroom and placed all of the dishes from the cupboard in one and all of the foodstuffs that I could fit into the other. *Surely the mice will not be able to get in there,* I determined as I closed the lids with a bang and marched over to my school, too upset to bother about breakfast.

By the time the students began to arrive, I had calmed down a bit and was able to welcome them with a smile.

The next two days went well, though it was a nuisance to be digging around in the trunks every time I fixed a meal.

On Wednesday, Lars brought me a fresh supply of produce and stared in amazement as I placed bread, cheese, and eggs in my large trunk.

"I have mice," I informed him as I went to place the milk, cream, and butter in the metal pail with a lid in the dugout on the north end of the house.

"Ya need a cat?" he asked, and I wondered why I hadn't thought of that.

"Do you have one that I could borrow?"

"Ve have lots. More all da time."

"I'll think about it."

We went to the classroom together.

On Thursday morning I awoke to find a drowned mouse in my slop bucket. I was horrified as I stared at the soggy lump of lifeless fur.

Well, at least it wasn't my water pail, I thought as I carried my slop bucket to the farthest corner of the school grounds and dumped it. I half expected the dead mouse to jump up and dash for my house but, fortunately, it stayed put. I turned and ran for the house myself.

I wanted to scrub out the slop bucket with soapy water, but that seemed foolish, so I just rinsed it a bit and set it a little farther away from my eating area. Again I skipped breakfast and went right to school.

That night I laid aside all of my reserve and headed over to the Petersons' to beg, borrow, or steal a cat.

The one that Lars offered me was rather mangy looking, a big, yellow thing.

"She be a good mouser," he maintained, and I didn't doubt him for a moment.

He carried her home for me—an act that I appreciated very much. I would rather have had one of the many cute little kittens, but Lars talked me out of that. "No good fer mice," he said. I took his word for it.

Lars deposited the large, hungry-looking cat in my kitchen and turned to go. "Vatch da door," he cautioned. "If she get out, she run home."

I watched the door. Lars left and the cat stayed.

Later I almost wished that she had gone. She prowled and yowled until I thought I wouldn't be able to stand another minute of it. Still, if she cleared my house of mice, the noise and commotion would be worth it.

At bedtime I shut my door against her nervous activity. I could hear her prowling and climbing, jumping and mewing, and I mentally followed her about the room—my chair, my table, my cupboard, my trunk. That cat didn't respect a single piece of furniture.

And then I heard a dreadful crash. *If that was my teapot!* was my first thought as I reached for a match to light the lamp. Fortunately, it was only a chipped cup that I had neglected to remove from the table. I swept up the broken pieces and dumped them into the stove. I took my teapot into the bedroom and carefully placed it in the trunk with my books. Then I blew out the lamp and crawled back into bed. I tried to force my thoughts away from the restless cat as it prowled about my house. *No mice will show tonight,* I thought, *with all of that racket going on.* I was wrong. About four in the morning I was awakened by a commotion in my kitchen, and then a sharp, sickening squeak of fright or pain. The cat had pounced.

The dreadful sound reverberated through my brain long after the cat had decided to call it a night. What an awful thing to be a small mouse caught by a mammoth cat!

In the morning my revulsion toward the incident hung over me like a cloud. I delayed getting up for as long as I dared. I was sure that I would find my kitchen strewn with dead mice. I didn't. Puss was still there, looking hungry and lean. There was no evidence of her nocturnal hunting.

I was nearing the conclusion that I must have imagined the sounds in the night when my tidying brought me to my favorite chair. At first I supposed that a small twig had somehow found its way onto the seat. I reached down and picked it up. It was in my hand before I recognized it—the tail of a mouse! The cat had dared to have her dinner right where I did my evening relaxing!

That did it. I went to my door, and feeling a little foolish, opened it slightly and called the cat. As she slinked out and started running for home, I asked forgiveness of the mice. Surely there was a more civilized way of getting rid of them. One thing I knew for sure: there must be a quieter way.

TWENTY

A Visitor

Before long, I was reminded again that I was still not rid of mice. I had no idea how many remained, but I judged it to be more than enough.

My cupboard stood empty while my trunks fairly bulged with what should have been on the shelves. Just making a cup of tea required extra effort. Those things that I couldn't fit into my trunks I covered. I covered my water pail. I even covered the spout of my teakettle. No matter what job I did, I checked first for the evidence of a mouse having been there before me. It was an awkward way to live, but I forced myself to adjust to it.

My pupils were progressing favorably. I had been assured that after the field work was finished, I would have three or four more students.

I was having a problem with Phillip Delaney. He tended to occupy himself with things other than what he was assigned to do. When, for three days running, his copy work was not completed by dismissal time, I asked him to stay for a chat after the pupils had been dismissed. I explained very carefully that should it happen again, I would require him to remain behind to finish his work.

The next day, to my dismay, his work was not completed.

"Phillip, I am disappointed," I said. "You had plenty of time to do your work."

He didn't seem concerned. "Shall I stay and do it like Tommy does?"

"Thomas needs special help with his lessons. He doesn't understand them on his own. That's why he stays, so that I can help him."

"But you said if I didn't finish, I'd have to stay."

"That's right."

He made no comment but reached for his pencil and began to work.

He finished his work quickly and then lingered until I insisted that he run home.

The next day his work went unfinished again.

"You'll have to stay until it's done," I declared. "Maybe this will help you to learn to work more quickly." I knew that Phillip's problem was not difficulty in understanding, for Phillip, unlike Thomas, was a bright child.

He did not protest. Again the work was done in good time, and again Phillip hung around chatting. I finally sent him home.

A short while later, I had an unexpected visitor. I was just putting away the last of the books that had been used in the day's lessons and was tidying up, when there was a rap on the door. Wynn Delaney walked in.

As usual, his presence unnerved me, and I expect that I flushed slightly.

"Am I interrupting?" he asked.

"Not at all. I was just leaving. Please come in."

He stepped to the front and took a seat near my desk. It looked odd to see such a tall man curled up in the small desk. He had to stretch his long legs out before him to make room for them. Somehow his relaxed attitude put me more at ease.

"More letters?" I asked mischievously.

He smiled and shook his head.

"No, this time it's school business. I came to see you about Phillip. He's had to stay after school a couple of times."

I thought, *What do you have to do with Phillip?* But I pushed it aside as the issue of my discipline being questioned seemed more important.

"You object to my method of discipline?"

"Not at all," he responded, almost as quickly. "I merely wonder if it's the best way to handle Phillip."

"Meaning?"

"Tell me, Miss Thatcher, how did Phillip respond to staying late? Did it upset him—annoy him?"

"Not at all." I was becoming defensive.

He smiled—a slow, deliberate smile, and in spite of myself I noticed what a pleasant smile he had. Yet his smile also told me that he had somehow just proved a point. He didn't even say anything; he just waited for me to understand what he had just said.

"You mean. . . ?" I began slowly.

"Exactly. Phillip likes nothing better than the extra time and attention, Miss Thatcher."

"I see," I said, looking away from him, realizing as I reviewed the past few days that he was quite right. I turned slowly back to him.

"So—" I began, reaching out for advice, "What do you suggest?"

"Well, his mother and I—"

His mother and I. The words hit me like a pail of cold water and I could feel the air leaving my lungs and the blood draining out of my head. For a moment I felt dizzy, and I lowered myself into my chair, not even checking first to make sure that it was really where it was supposed to be. *His mother and I—Delaney . . . of course, Phillip Delaney—Wynn Delaney.* This was Phillip's father. *What a fool I've been,* I upbraided myself, *to be nursing illusions about a married man.*

I recovered quickly as I realized that Mr. Delaney was waiting for my response to his suggestion, which I had missed in my dismay.

"I'm sorry—" I stumbled along awkwardly, "I'm afraid my thoughts . . . I—I was off somewhere and I didn't—"

I left it dangling and he repeated, "His mother and I thought that if you could send uncompleted work home with him, we would see that it was finished and returned."

"Of course." I felt embarrassed that he had to explain again.

It seemed like a good enough plan. And right now I was willing to agree with almost anything that would speed this man's departure from my schoolroom.

I stood up and hurried on, "That sounds like a good approach. I will tell Phillip of the new arrangement. And now if—if you'll excuse me, Mr. Delaney, I do have things—a lot of things to attend to."

He arose with a questioning look in his eyes; I then remembered I had told him when he entered that I was finished and ready to leave. He did not mention the fact, however, and excused himself in a gentlemanly fashion.

Odd feelings were quivering within me as I watched him go. What a silly goose I had been to blithely assume that he was unmarried. The fact that he was the most attractive man I had ever met I could not deny—but had I known he was married, I never would have allowed him another thought. *Well, I know now—so that is that,* I thought mentally, giving myself a shake. I firmly pushed all thoughts of the man from me and walked briskly from the classroom. I decided to run over to Anna's for a cup of her good, strong coffee. She was always coaxing me to come, and I too often pleaded busyness. Well, tonight I would take time. I was in no mood to sit by myself and calmly sip tea. *I might even stay for supper if she insists,* I told myself, knowing full well that she would. *It will save me standing on my head to dig something from my trunks,* and thus keeping my thoughts in control, I resolutely shut the door behind me.

TWENTY-ONE
Pupils

Only once did Phillip need to have work sent home with him. He gave it to me the next morning, carefully completed. From then on, Phillip finished his work easily in the allotted time.

He was a little charmer. I suppose that, try as I might not to, I must have shown a slight amount of favoritism. He found little ways to spend time with me, and I'm sure that I enjoyed it every bit as much as he did.

Else Peterson was also one of my "special" students. She was quick to learn and eager to please. I did have opportunity to have her for Saturday "tea." That day she had run across the field between us with some warm coffeecake, fresh from her mother's oven. It was delicious, and we called it "tea" cake instead, eating it right away with our tea served in my china cups. Else's tea, diluted with milk, was a marvelous treat for her, and her eyes sparkled through her shyness as she looked at the cups and the dainty teapot.

"Miss T'atcher," she told me solemnly, "it is like having a fairy picnic."

I loved little Else. She was a precious, gentle child.

Sally Clark also found a warm place in my heart. She was rather pathetic, this girl-turning-woman. She wanted so much to enter into the adult world, yet she clung to her childish world as well. I noticed, as the days went by, her shy watching of me and her awkward attempts to copy me. I took it as a sincere compliment, and I often wished that I could take her home with me and put her in one of my pretty dresses, arrange her hair, and then let her see the attractive girl in the mirror. She was a pretty girl in her own way, and I often had the impression that someday we might waken and find this shy little butterfly free of her cocoon. I realized that I would be unwise to try and rush nature's own slow, yet certain, process. To show Sally through my wardrobe and tempt her with pretty things that I had always taken for granted would only make her worn and simple clothing look all the more drab in her eyes. So, rather, I made simple suggestions and spoke words of encouragement when I could: "Blue is one of your best colors"; "That type of collar suits you well"; "Your hair looks very pretty that way—you have such pretty hair." I tried to build up each one of my pupils with sincere praise, but with Sally my smiles and words had extra meaning. She flushed slightly when I did this, but I knew that my approval was important to her.

Then there was Andy. Even to look at him made my heart ache. He seemed to grow worse as the days went by. At times I saw him reach up and grasp his head with both hands as though he were in pain, a look of confusion and misery filling his eyes. I tried not to draw attention to him, but as soon as I was able I'd come to his side and kneel beside him.

"Andy, why don't you just put your head down on your arms for a few minutes," I would whisper.

What I truly longed to do was gather him into my own arms and shelter him there, though I seldom had the appropriate opportunity. Usually he would look at me with thankfulness in his eyes, and then he would do as I suggested, sometimes rocking himself gently back and forth. I was concerned that his inability to cope with the schoolwork might be causing him physical problems. I did not push him, but I did so want to offer him all that he was capable of retaining. I was on the verge of trying to find out where he lived so that I could call on his folks when, one school morning, Andy did not arrive with his sister Teresa.

"Mamma think he need rest," she said, and I nodded my head in sympathetic agreement.

All the students missed Andy. He was a favorite with everyone, for even though he could not fully participate in classroom learning or outside games, he vigorously cheered on all who could. In the classroom his eyes would shine whenever anyone read or recited well, and occasionally he spontaneously clapped his hands in jolly appreciation. I never reproached him for his exuberance, and the students watched Andy as they recited, hoping to win his favor. On the playground he watched the games with intent, and shouted and jumped wildly for any accomplishment. Andy did not pick favorites. He cheered everyone on with the same enthusiasm. His clapping hands and fervent exclamation of, "You did good! You did good!" was something that each student worked for.

Carl Clark, just entering his teens, was a problem for me. He was Sally's cousin and made it known that he didn't need this "dumb ol' school"—he was going to be a cowboy and work on a ranch in southern Alberta. He spent far more time practicing with his lariat than poring over his reader. He spent every recess roping fence posts.

He had started out roping fellow students until I had firmly put a stop to it.

One day I gave Harvey Mattoch, one of my younger children, permission to leave the room; and, as I did with all of my children, I kept an eye out for his return. The minutes ticked by, and still no Harvey. I went on with the spelling lesson, but my mind kept wondering about Harvey. When I dismissed the class for recess, I immediately went to look for him. I found him cowering behind the woodpile in tears.

"Harvey," I coaxed, "come on out and let's talk about it."

He shook his head, and a fresh torrent of tears began to fall.

"What happened?"

He cried harder.

I sat down on a block of wood and waited for his outburst to subside. As soon as he seemed to have control, I passed him my handkerchief, let him mop up and blow his nose, then asked him again.

"The—the door to—to the boys' place is all tied up," he managed between sobs.

Sure enough, it was—with Carl Clark's lariat. Harvey had tried to get the rope untied and the door free, but not in time to avert an "accident." I gave him permission to run home for dry clothes.

"You stay right here out of sight," I told him, "until I call the children in from recess. No one else has missed you yet."

I wrote a quick note to his mother in the hope that the boy wouldn't be scolded or shamed at home, smuggled it to him, and then rang the bell. A few minutes later I saw the bobbing of his head as he ran down the road in his hurry to get home unnoticed.

At the end of the day I asked Carl to remain behind. I told him how disappointed I was that he would use his rope to tie up a *needed* building and that for the next week his recesses would be occupied in hauling wood for the school stove. I also told him that his lariat was not to be seen at school again. He sulked as he left the room, but I had no further problem with the rope. Eventually Carl even joined the other boys in their games. I did have to revise my recess punishment, however. The weather had been too mild to use the big iron stove, and Carl hauled enough wood in two days to completely fill the wood storage bin in the schoolhouse and stack more by the door.

Considering the fact that my students had never had any formal education prior to this year; considering the fact that I had very few educational aids to use on their behalf; considering the fact that I had all of them under one roof and on all grade levels; considering the fact that they came from various ethnic backgrounds, and some of them did not even speak English well; considering the fact that I was young with only two previous years of teaching experience, I was rather proud of everyone—well, almost everyone.

During the weeks that followed I had the pleasant experience of being invited to several neighborhood homes for Sunday dinner or a weekday supper. Some of the homes I visited were even more simply furnished than my little teacherage. A few were surprisingly comfortable and charmingly decorated and arranged. But wherever I went, the people were anxious to share with me the best they could offer. I loved them for it.

It was difficult for me to accept their hospitality when I was not in a position to return it. They seemed to sense how I felt and were quick to assure me that this was their small way of saying thanks to me for coming to teach their children. It made me more determined than ever to do the best that I could.

TWENTY-TWO

The School Stove

Very suddenly the warm weather turned cold and rainy. One morning I awoke to a cloudy, dark sky, a cold wind, and rain like ice water. Even in my snug little house I shivered as I dressed. I could hardly believe that a day could be so drastically different from the one just preceding. it. I decided that my schoolroom must have a fire—the first one yet needed. At least we were well stocked for wood, thanks to Carl.

As I looked at the sky, I was glad that it was Friday. Maybe by Monday we'd have our sunshine back again.

I built my own fire and put on my coffeepot. The hungry flames began to lick at the wood quickly, and the warmth was soon spilling out into the room. As I looked at the dismal day, I wondered how many of my students would venture forth. I wouldn't have blamed them if they'd stayed home.

I decided to do everything that was necessary before leaving the house so that once I had crossed to the schoolhouse in the rain I could stay there.

With this in mind, I cared for my daily grooming, almost gasping for breath as I washed in the cold water; I breakfasted, had my morning Bible reading, and tidied my two small rooms. Before I left I banked my fire the way that Lars had shown me and then bundled myself up tightly in my coat, tied a scarf on my head, and dashed for the school.

It was cold in the room, all right, but I still had plenty of time to take the chill from the air before my students arrived.

I threw aside my coat and went to work on laying the firewood. My hands were already numb with the cold and dampness. I got the paper and kindling ready to light but, though I searched everywhere that a matchbox might be, I found none. I buttoned on my coat, donned my damp scarf, and dashed back through the rain to the teacherage for some matches. In my haste as I returned to the school, I stepped into a big puddle and splashed muddy water up my leg. Undaunted, I ran on and, once inside, threw off my coat and dripping scarf and went to work on the fire again. I had no problem getting the kindling to accept the flame and soon a brisk fire was begging greedily for more fuel; also, soon the room was beginning to fill with blue woodsmoke. I opened the door of the stove and peered in. Smoke puffed out and stung my eyes. I slammed the door shut. *Maybe it will take just a few moments to begin to draw,* I thought, thinking of my father's words concerning our fireplace at home.

The minutes passed by, and the stove did *not* draw; it only seemed to *blow*—billows of choking smoke filled the classroom.

I poked and fussed with the fire, but it only increased my coughing and watering eyes and got soot and ashes all over my hands and clothing. Determining that the only way to save my room from total disaster was to drench the fire, I picked up the pail of water. I was about to heave it into the stove when the school door opened and there stood Wynn Delaney. I gasped, choked, and began another fit of coughing.

Without speaking he crossed to me, took the pail from my hands and set it back on its shelf. Then he moved on to the stove.

"These country school stoves can be contrary things," he stated matter-of factly as he flipped some metal lever on the stove pipe and another on the stove itself. Then he walked purposefully to the windows and began to open them one by one. After the last one had been flung wide, he returned and picked up my coat.

"I have a few minutes," he offered. "Why don't I stay and tend the fire while you go on home and freshen up. It'll be a good forty minutes before any students appear."

He held my coat for me, and I shrugged into it without speaking. I fled from the building in embarrassment at being discovered in such a predicament. What a mess I was! I had soot streaks up my arms and even across my cheek. My legs and dress were splattered with mud, my shoes were soggy, and my hair was tumbling down. I eyed the clock as I scrubbed and changed but I did not hurry. I even had a second cup of coffee, feeling a bit like a child stealing from the cookie jar. I then slowly and deliberately picked my way across the yard to the schoolhouse, skirting all of the deeper puddles. By the time I reached the school, most of the smoke had cleared, and the room was beginning to warm with the cheerily burning—and smokeless—fire. My benefactor was still there.

In spite of my embarrassment, my sense of humor held me in good stead, at least in measure.

"I want to thank you," I began, "for rescuing the schoolhouse. We nearly went up in smoke."

When he saw that I could laugh at myself, his eyes began to twinkle, but he was too kind to tease me.

"Someone," he said, placing all the blame on an unknown and unseen "someone," "left the damper completely closed." He stepped over to the stove and turned the damper lever slightly. "When the fire gets going well, you can turn it—like this—to slow it down some; but to start with, it should always be turned upright, like this."

I nodded, berating myself for not thinking of dampers. He didn't remark about my folly, though, but went on, "I must warn you, though, don't *ever* use a full pail of water to douse a fire in a stove like this. It can be very dangerous—and at best, very messy. The water forces the ashes, some of them carrying live sparks, to blow out through the stove door."

A mental image of the forcefully splashing water, the flying ashes and soot made me thankful that he had come in when he did.

"If you must quench a fire," he continued, "*gently* pour on water, a dipperful at a time, working your way over the flames. Remember, too, it doesn't take long for an iron stove to heat; a sudden change in temperature might even split the metal."

I nodded meekly, feeling that I had just been given a fatherly lecture on fires.

"Never did hold to this business of a young woman teacher having to care for her own fire," he remarked, as though to himself. I cringed inwardly as I imagined him at some future meeting of the parents in the community, taking his stand to argue that young women teachers had no business caring for the fire in the classroom.

I quickly assured him, "It'll be fine, now that I know how it operates."

He threw two more good-sized chunks of wood on the flames, closed the door of the stove and straightened to his full height. I saw his eyes fall to my hands, and I became more self-conscious and nervous. Was he noticing that my hands showed I was not used to manual work of any kind? Was he checking to see if they were losing their cared-for look under the rigors of work in a country school?

I moved to a window.

"Do you suppose we can close them now?" I asked in an effort to direct his attention elsewhere.

"Certainly," and he moved to the nearest one.

I looked around my room and as soon as the last window had been closed, I turned to him.

"I do want to thank you—and I will remember to check the damper. Now, if you'll excuse me, I have lessons to prepare."

He smiled slightly and reached for his hat. It was strange, this feeling I had. I knew instinctively that he was the kind of man who would be worthy of anyone's friendship, especially since he was a longtime friend of Jonathan's; yet I felt that I dared not encourage a friendship of any kind. I had never felt such a barrier, or rather the need for such a barrier, with a man before. Perhaps I feared lest he somehow was aware of my attraction to him before I had realized that he was a married man. Perhaps if I met his wife I would be able to feel differently. But for now I held myself stiffly at a distance.

"I stopped to let you know that Phillip won't be attending class today. He has a cold, and his mother has decided not to send him out in the rain."

At the words "his mother," I backed away a step farther from the man who spoke to me.

"I'm—I'm sorry," I managed. "I do hope that it will not be serious."

"I'm sure that it won't. You know children. They can be back racing about in an hour's time. Mothers take a little longer to recuperate from a child's illness." He grinned.

"Yes," I answered. "I guess so."

"I'll be coming back this way sometime between three and four. Lydia would like me to pick up Phillip's work so that he won't fall behind his classmates. She'll go over the lesson with him at home—if that's not too much trouble for you."

"No—no, of course not. I'll have it ready for you when you come by."

He smiled again, nodded slightly, and left, his hat still in his hand. I turned to my blackboard, trying hard to concentrate on the lessons that I had to prepare. I dreaded the day ahead, for I knew that at its end I must see him again. I wished that I could keep Lars with me, to send him out to meet this man and hand him the required lessons. Of course I knew that I couldn't do that. Lars was needed at home and, anyway, I would not hold any student for such a foolish and personal reason. With time and effort I would get over my silly feelings and accept the man as Jon's married male friend—nothing more. He had never behaved as other than a perfect gentleman in my presence.

To my amazement, all of my students except Phillip and Andy appeared for class. In fact, the total number that day was swelled, for the three older boys who had been working in the harvest fields were released because of the rain and attended classes for the first time.

It soon became apparent, much to my consternation and embarrassment, that it was the young schoolmarm, rather than the lessons, who had brought them; they were not much younger than

I and took every opportunity to tease and flirt a bit. I felt my cheeks flush several times during the day and was thankful when this awkward school day was finally over.

Immediately, I set to work in preparing the material for Phillip's home lessons. I did not want Mr. Delaney to be required to stand around waiting for them.

The students had not been gone long and I had just finished my hurried preparations when his knock sounded on the schoolroom door.

I gave him the packet, which he tucked inside his jacket to protect it from the rain, and then I dismissed him—rather curtly, I'm afraid.

"I must get home and tend to my fire," I told him, and hurried into my coat as I said the words. I made sure that I stood far enough away from him that he couldn't offer assistance.

He looked at me, then out the window, then at my flimsy shoes.

"I could take you across on my horse," he offered as I moved toward the door.

I stopped in mid-stride. What a perfectly ridiculous idea! *And how does he propose to do that?* He must have read my shock.

"It's knee-deep out there in places."

Anger took hold of me now. I forgot to think of him as Jon's friend and thought of him only as some woman's husband.

I inwardly fumed. *Here he is, wanting to transport me home on his horse. How would he do that—fling me across its back, or carry me in his arms?*

"I'll manage," I declared, and he didn't argue further. He left with Phillip's homework, and in frustration I stamped about the classroom, putting away books, erasing the blackboard, and shoving desks into line.

At length I calmed down and went out to face the storm, careful to close the classroom door tightly behind me.

As the cold rain whipped into my face, I became more clearheaded. I reminded myself that Mr. Delaney was a longtime friend of my brother Jonathan. His offer to deliver me home on his horse was a simple courtesy—out of a desire to care for the helpless young sister of a man whom he considered almost a brother; his thoughtful offer was nothing more than that. I felt better having sorted it out in my thinking. Perhaps Lydia Delaney's husband merely was overly helpful, and she need have no worries after all. I put the whole thing from my mind and began to plan a comfortable and restful evening.

Mr. Delaney had been right—the water was deep. By the time I reached my door my shoes were ruined, my skirts were covered with muddy water, and my spirits were as soggy as my wet-to-the-knees hose.

But I refused to mope about for the evening. My little ritual with teacup, familiar chair, and a favorite Dickens story went a long way toward improving my outlook.

TWENTY-THREE

Plans

Saturday was also cold and rainy. I hand-washed my laundry and strung lines around my house to dry it. In the afternoon I had to haul more wood. It was a wet, muddy job, and I didn't enjoy it.

Sunday, too, was wet and miserable. Few people turned out for the afternoon service. Lars came over early to start the fire in the school stove. It did not smoke. Those who gathered were glad for its warmth and cheeriness. As previously arranged with Mr. Dickerson, I welcomed the children into the teacherage where we had a special Bible story, so I did not have much opportunity to visit with the other worshipers. Mr. Delaney was there with his mother, a very sweet-looking person, and when I met her I realized from whom Mr. Delaney had inherited his warm, friendly smile. Phillip was still homebound with his cold, so his mother had stayed at home with him.

After the service and my class was over, I escorted the children to the school, bid farewell to the worshipers, checked the stove in the classroom, and sloshed home through the puddles. The rain had now stopped, and the sun was reappearing. Soon the earth was steaming from the heat. Fortunately, it looked as if our present spell of bad weather would be short-lived.

By midweek the yard and roads were dry again. On Wednesday our other "sun" returned; Andy was back. The whole class cheered for him as he entered the schoolyard. I was just going out to ring the bell when he appeared, and I must admit that I, too, wished to cheer when I saw his sparkling eyes. His joy at being back lit his whole face.

By midmorning I could tell that something was very wrong, but

Andy shook his head when I asked him if he'd like to rest his head on his arms. By afternoon the pain dulled his eyes, and even resting his head didn't help. I called Teresa aside and suggested that she take him home.

"He shouldn't come," she said anxiously, "but he been so sad, an' he coax an' coax."

We bundled him up. They didn't live far from the school, but I was anxious as I let him go, praying that he would be able to make it home.

Just as Andy and Teresa moved out the door, Carl Clark's hand shot up. He didn't even wait to be recognized, something that I usually insisted upon. "Teacher," he said quickly, "how 'bout I go along? Andy might need some carryin'."

There was real concern in Carl's eyes, and my appreciation and relief must have shown on my face. Silently I nodded my permission.

The entire class watched the three of them leave. The silence was broken by Else's whisper, "He's real sick, ain't he, Teacher?"

Swallowing over the lump in my throat, I could only nod. I even ignored the "ain't."

"His folks should've taken him to the doctor again," Mindy Blake commented.

"They ain't got no money." This from Lars, my star grammar student, his frustration apparent in his voice and choice of words.

"Then we should help them," offered the shy Olga. She rarely spoke out in class.

"Us? How?" replied many voices.

Olga withdrew in embarrassment. Her seatmate, Maudie Clark, put a protective hand on her arm and then spoke boldly. "It wasn't a dumb idea. We could, you know. We could bring our nickels and dimes or pennies even—an' do special things at home so our pa's might give us more money. An' then we could put it together an'—"

"Nickels an' pennies don't pay a doctor none." This from Mike Clark.

"They'd help." Maudie wasn't going to back down. I decided to get things back under control.

"I'm glad that in your concern for Andy, you're willing to do something to help him, and I think that it's a good idea—and a workable one. I'm sure that there is some way that we can find . . ." My words hung for a moment. It did sound possible. I just wasn't sure yet how to go about it.

"I want you to think about this tonight—all of you. What might we be able to do? Ask your parents for ideas. And tomorrow when we come, we'll discuss our ideas and see what we can do."

All of the faces before me brightened. We settled back to our studies, but I often caught pensive looks and muffled whispers; I knew that thoughts were still on Andy and a possible way that we might help in getting him the medical attention he needed.

I still had not solved my mice problem; my declaration of war daily seemed more impossible. The mice were not content with peaceful coexistence or with taking over my entire cupboard, having driven me to my trunks; but they wanted the rest of my house as well. Every time I cleaned up after them, my anger increased.

On Friday morning it was apparent that they had enjoyed a good night's romp. For the first time I found evidence that they had joined me in my bedroom. This was too much. Already in a foul mood after seeing where they had been, I went to the top drawer of my chest to get a fresh handkerchief. I hadn't noticed it before, but the drawer had been open slightly because of a glove that had caught. Meticulous about closing drawers, I wondered how this one had missed my attention.

I laid the glove properly in its section of the drawer and reached in the handkerchief box. Before my hand touched one of them, my eyes flashed me a message. Something was wrong—seriously wrong, and then I realized what had happened. The mice had been at my handkerchiefs! With a cry I pulled them out and stared at them. Pretty lace and embroidery had been reduced to chewed fragments. My favorite handkerchief, with the daintiest lace that I had ever seen, had suffered the worst. It was beyond repair, and frustrated tears gathered in my eyes and rolled down my cheeks as I looked at it. Angrily I returned the box to the drawer, slammed the drawer shut, and marched off to the classroom. This time the mice had gone too far!

After class I planned to call on the school-board chairman, Mr. Laverly, and insist that someone, somehow, dispose of those despicable rodents. I would refuse to live in the teacherage until something was done.

By the time the students had arrived, I had managed to quiet my anger. We began our day by saluting our flag and reading some verses of scripture. I realized as the class took their seats that it would not do to go directly to our lessons. Their excited faces told me that first we must discuss what we as a school could do to help Andy.

Many suggestions were presented, some to cheers and others to groans. I listed them all carefully on the board. I wrote in large letters, realizing that Tim Mattoch had an eye problem and could hardly see the board. His parents could not afford to get him glasses, so Tim struggled on, squinting and squirming, often having to approach the board so that he might make out a letter or a number.

There were many good suggestions. I decided to let the students discuss them for a few minutes before we commenced our lessons. After a fair amount of discussion, Mindy suggested that we take a vote. It seemed reasonable. The voters decided that we would have a penny circus and a box social on October twenty-fifth at the school; all money raised through the event would go to help Andy Pastachuck. Everyone was happy and excited, but once the matter was decided, they were better able to settle down to their lessons. I was proud of them for their concern, and I was also eager to help Andy in any way that we could.

At the end of the day I asked for the directions to the Laverlys' farm. The place would not be hard to find but required a three-mile walk. Undaunted, I put on my hat, buttoned my coat, and set off. For the first two miles I walked with the Clark girls. The boys had hurried on ahead, for they had chores awaiting them. Also, they didn't care to be seen with a bunch of girls. The Blake girls had also walked with us for the first mile.

It was a pleasant day, and I found the little expedition enjoyable. Only a few mudholes remained in the road from the recent heavy rain, and those we were easily able to skirt.

After I left my students, I walked more briskly. I missed their chatter, but on the other hand I was glad for the solitude after a busy school day. At last the Laverly farm came into view.

The Laverly sons were no longer of school age, and I thought that it was very commendable of Mr. Laverly to have worked so hard to get a school when none of his family would directly benefit from it.

Mrs. Laverly was a bustling, energetic woman with a great deal of curiosity. She pumped me with questions, not only about my work in the classroom but about my family and background as well. She insisted that I have coffee and sandwiches. After she had set the pot on to boil, she went to the back porch and pounded with a metal rod on a large iron plate. I jumped at the first loud, harsh sound.

"Thet'll call in the menfolk," she explained, "They're in the field out back."

I apologized for interrupting Mr. Laverly from his work. I hadn't even considered that he might be busy, so anxious was I to be rid of my freeloading tenants.

"Thet's a'right. Thet's a'right," she assured me. "They'll be wantin' somethin' to eat anyway. An' b'sides, it's time for one of 'em to start chorin'."

Mrs. Laverly set to work on a huge plate of man-sized sandwiches. Thick slices of homemade bread, generously—though not particularly carefully—spread with fresh butter and covered with large portions of cheese or cold roast beef were quickly assembled, while her tongue moved as fast as her hands. I wondered if I'd be able to get such thick sandwiches into my mouth. I offered to help her, but she waved me off with the butcher knife that she was using on the beef.

"No need to be a helpin'. Me, I'm not used to another woman underfoot. Had to do it alone all my life. Jest raised boys, ya know—five of 'em. Lost one, but still got four. One of 'em's married an' lives near Edmonton. Other three lives right here an' helps with the farm. Don't know what their pa would do without 'em. Middle one's kinda got 'im a girl, an' the youngest one's been a'lookin'. Oldest one don't seem much interested. S'pose I'll end up havin' to find someone for 'im an' draggin' 'im off to the preacher myself."

She rambled on as if it were one continuous sentence with hardly a pause for breath.

The sandwiches were placed on the table, and tin cups for coffee were set out. We could hear the menfolk tramping toward the house. They stopped on the back porch to slosh water over their faces and arms, squabbled some over the rights to the coarse towel, brushed the worst of the straw from themselves, and came in.

It was apparent from their faces that they hadn't expected to see me. Three grown men suddenly turned shy. One of them flushed beet red, while another fiddled nervously with his hair, his collar, his suspenders. The third one seemed to regain his composure almost immediately and decided to make the most of the situation, appearing to take pleasure in the discomfort of his brothers. He turned out to be George, the middle one, the one with a girl. The red-faced one was Bill, the youngest; the nervous one was the eldest son, Henry. I recognized them as three of the men who had huddled near the door during my welcoming party.

We sat up to the table together, and the men reached for the sandwiches, the enormous size giving them no pause. I managed, too, in spite of the fact that the portions were anything but dainty; they were delicious, especially after my nice, long walk.

Mr. Laverly was cordial and warm. He was even allowed to ask me a question or two in between the ones peppered at me by Mrs.

Laverly. The three sons were at first too busy with eating to pay any attention to the conversation—or so I thought. By the time the supper was over, George was joking and teasing, and Bill was openly staring. But Henry kept his eye on his plate and cup, unwilling—or unable—to participate in the talk around the table.

I waited until after the meal—for it was a complete meal by my standards—before I asked to talk to Mr. Laverly concerning my mice problem. He was such a nice man that I approached the subject very calmly, making sure I didn't insinuate that the mice were inhabiting the teacherage with his permission. I hurriedly poured out my whole tale. He stuffed his pipe and lit it, inhaled a few times, but all of the time that I talked, he offered no comment. I told him of the mice dwelling in my cupboards, entering into my bedroom, and taking over my dresser drawers. However, I did not tell him about my lace handkerchiefs. I was afraid that if I went into those details I would lose my temper, or cry—or maybe both.

He listened patiently, but eventually I gathered that he felt that a few mice in the house were really nothing to get so worked up about. When I finally stopped for breath, he removed the pipe from his mouth.

"We'll git ya some traps."

"I tried that."

He looked surprised.

"Well, a cat might—"

"I tried that, too," I said in frustration. I avoided explaining *why* they hadn't worked.

"Me an' the boys'll go over an' see what we can find. Must be comin' in somewhere. We'll take some tin an' nail up the holes."

This sounded good, but I was not completely satisfied.

"What about those that are already in?" I asked.

"We'll care fer 'em."

I was more content then.

"Hope ya don't mind us stirrin' round in yer quarters none. We'll git at it this next week."

I thought of the silent Henry, the teasing George, and the flirting Bill.

"Perhaps it would be best if I moved out for the week."

"Moved out?" He looked alarmed, as though if I left the teacherage, he might never see me again.

"To the Petersons. Anna has already told me that should I ever need a room, she could spare one."

He looked relieved.

"Good idea," he said and removed his pipe. He shook the ashes into the coal bucket and laid the pipe back on the shelf, as though to indicate that the matter was closed.

I went back to the kitchen to thank Mrs. Laverly for the supper. She was busy wrapping a portion of the cold meat and a jar of her pickles for me to take home.

"The boys have gone fer the team," she said.

At my questioning look, she explained, "Too late fer ya to start out a'walkin'. One of 'em will drive ya." She began to chuckle. "Saw 'em a'flippin' fer it."

I wondered who would be taking me—the winner or the loser of the toss. I found myself trying to decide which one I hoped it would be.

The lucky—or unlucky—one was Bill. He came in grinning from ear to ear, announcing that he was ready any time I was. Bill—the one who was "a'lookin'." I smiled rather weakly, I'm afraid, and followed him out. He didn't offer to help me up, so I scrambled over the wagon wheel on my own, dragging my skirts and clutching my food parcels. Then we were off.

The team was spirited and Bill liked speed, which didn't enhance the comfort of the rough wagon. Bill muttered over and over about "havin' to talk to Pa 'bout a light buggy." Jostling along, trying to cling to my precarious perch, I felt sure that the sweating team, and all of Bill's future passengers, would approve of a lighter vehicle for traveling at such a pace.

My main concern was staying on the wagon seat. I had to hold onto the brown paper bag containing my cold beef and pickles, so

I clutched the edge, white-knuckled, with the other hand. By the time we reached the teacherage, my bones felt like I had been trampled. I clambered slowly down over the wheel, wondering if my legs would still hold me when my feet reached the ground.

Bill, removing neither himself from his seat nor his hat from his head, seemed rather pleased with himself, as though he had perhaps made the run in record time. I felt sure that he had. He grinned at me, and I knew that he expected me to appreciate his feat.

"Thank you for bringing me home," I said shakily. "It—it was very kind of you."

Bill's grin widened.

"Next time, maybe I'll have me a buggy. Then we won't be held back by this ol' lumber wagon."

I hoped there would be no "next time," but I said nothing. Bill wheeled the horses around and left the yard at a near gallop. I shook my head, waved the dust away from my face, and turned to go into my house.

Tonight I would pack for my move to the Petersons and tuck everything else away, safe from the mice. I would go over right after my evening meal the next day, if this worked out for Anna.

"You'd better enjoy yourselves tonight," I warned the little varmints. "It might be your last chance."

From the evidence I found the next morning, it appeared they had.

TWENTY-FOUR

Napoleon

My week at the Petersons' went by quickly. I enjoyed the company of Anna and the cheerful chatter of the children. Even Olga warmed up to me somewhat when the two of us were alone.

On Friday, Bill Laverly stopped by the schoolhouse, grinning his wide grin, and assured me that the teacherage was now mouse-proof and mouse-free.

I decided that I would move back on Saturday morning so that I could spend the day scrubbing and cleaning and putting the things back into my cupboard.

Bill offered to drive me over to the Petersons' for my things. I was quick to assure him that I had taken very little with me and would have no problem carrying it home. I thanked him for his kindness and returned to my classroom.

Moving back home posed no difficulty. Olga and Else came with me, insisting on helping me carry my belongings. After they had left, I changed into an old skirt and shirtwaist and set to work with hot, soapy water. It gave me great satisfaction to see gleaming clean cupboards restored to their proper order.

I was tired at day's end but deeply pleased with my labors. It was good to be home and have my little house all to myself.

The area harvest was nearing completion. Some of the farmers were already finished. The older boys had now come back to the classroom, making my days more difficult. They longed to be adults and yet they did not have the skills of even the youngest children in the room. My heart ached for them, but they did try my patience to the limit. Their attempts to flirt annoyed me, and at times I had to suppress a strong desire to express my displeasure. I knew that they were immature and unsure of themselves, so I tried very hard never to embarrass or humiliate them. But I did wish that they wouldn't act so silly.

We were all busily involved in planning for the coming box social and penny circus. Assignments had been given to the students, and they were working hard to prepare for the big event. The parents were wonderful in their support. Almost daily, some note of encouragement or offer of help was brought to school by a student. I was pleased and thankful for the community backing.

On the home front, I felt rather smug: There had been no evidence whatever of mice in my kitchen. The tin patches in my cupboard and around the walls seemed to have done the trick. I did not know—nor ask—how the men had taken care of the unwelcome inhabitants. I was simply glad that they had been removed.

I was weary by Friday night. The older boys had been particularly trying, and the week had been filled with many extra duties for the upcoming fund-raiser. After I had cleared away my supper dishes, I retired to my large chair (the lumps were now fitting nicely around me) with a cup of tea and a book. I slipped off my shoes and put my feet up on my footstool. How my mother would have gasped to see her daughter sitting in such an unladylike position, but it felt *so* good. I sighed contentedly, sipped hot tea, and opened my book.

A tiny movement near the stove caught my eye. The bit of shadow turned into a live thing—a tiny mouse poked out his head. His black, shiny eyes sought out any danger and his nose twitched sensitively. My first angry impulse was to pick up my shoe and throw it at him, but I froze where I was. Venturing out a little farther, he sat up and began to clean himself, rubbing his tiny moistened paws over his head, his back, and his chest. He did look comical. He also looked small and helpless and hungry. I had never actually seen one of my house guests before—alive, that is. *He IS rather cute,* I reasoned, though there had been nothing much to commend them when they were dead.

I must have stirred slightly, for he darted back under the stove and was lost in the shadows.

He appeared a few more times that evening, each time carefully grooming himself. I wondered if this were just an attempt to keep himself busy and his thoughts off his empty tummy.

Before I went to bed, I scattered a few crumbs by the leg of the stove. I told myself that I was doing it to provide what he needed so he wouldn't have to climb into my cupboard looking for it. In the morning the crumbs were gone.

In the next few days, very busy days, I saw the small mouse on several occasions. I named him Napoleon because he was so tiny, yet so bold. Each night I put a small amount of food out for him, each time reasoning that if he had food easily accessible he wouldn't snoop in my cupboards for it.

I found myself actually watching for him. He was entertaining, and I even had the ridiculous thought that I no longer bore the loneliness of living by myself.

During school on Friday, a knock on the classroom door drew my attention. I excused myself and went to answer it. Bill Laverly had been to town and picked up some articles that I had requested for the penny circus. I told him to set them inside the door of the teacherage, then went back to my class, anxious for the school hours to end so that I could get busy on my projects.

Bill was soon back at the classroom door.

"Ma'am," he said, "there was another mouse in yer place there. Don't know how we ever missed 'im."

At the sight of my chalk-white face he hurried on, "It's okay, ma'am—I killed 'im."

My gratitude expected, I mumbled something that I hoped made sense, and Bill left, his eternal grin firmly in place.

It was a few moments before I could go back to my class. I knew that it was right—that it was better—that it was what I *should* have wanted. But I'd miss Napoleon. He had been so little, and so clever—and so cute.

TWENTY-FIVE

The Box Social

When the day of the Box Social arrived, my students were all so excited that they could scarcely think of another thing. They spent the morning attempting to finish their lessons, and devoted the entire afternoon to getting ready for the big event.

The older boys strung wire across the room, and the girls pinned old blankets and sheets on the wires, thus forming small booths. Within each booth a game, contest, or entertainment was set up by each of the students who had been put in charge. Excitement ran high, and it was hard for me to hold them all in check. At last we had done all that we could do in preparation, and they were dismissed to go home.

I circled the room, checking and rearranging. The students had done a fine job on their projects. It looked as if the night would be great fun as well as a help to the Pastachucks. There was a ring-toss, a fish pond, pin-the-tail-on-the-donkey, a mock camera, some pins to knock over, a pail-and-candy-toss game, and a bean-sack toss. Each game would cost the player a penny.

Our main source of income was to be our box social. I had spent two evenings decorating my box and had sent to town for special food items to prepare for the lunch to fill it. Each woman and older girl would have a decorated box filled with enough lunch for two people—although the lunch stuffed into some boxes would feed many more.

Mr. Dickerson had agreed to be our auctioneer. The men would bid on the boxes, and the highest bidder would share the food with the lady whose box he had purchased. I wondered who would end up being my partner for the evening's lunch. It was harmless enough to sit in a roomful of people, eating together. I was not concerned about the evening—only curious.

"Mama showed Pa *her* box," Mindy Blake had declared.

"She shouldn't've," said Maudie Clark.

"Well, she did," said Mindy in a huff. "She had to make 'nough for all us kids, ya know, an' she wouldn't want any ol' man gettin' all that."

"All you're worried 'bout, Mindy, is the food," Carl Clark accused.

"Boy, I should git me thet box," cut in Tim Mattoch, and everyone laughed. Tim was more than a little on the heavy side, and all of the students knew that he dearly loved to eat.

"He'll buy the biggest box there," said Mike Clark.

"He better not," Else interrupted, " 'cause it'll be my ma's. She had to pack for all of us kids, too, and she put it all togeder in a great big box, dis big." She indicated how big the box was and then immediately clamped her hand over her mouth, realizing that she had divulged a secret.

As I prepared my lunch, I was glad I didn't need to fix one for a whole family; but I also knew that some of those hard-working single males of our community were hearty eaters. It would not do to short-change them.

The wagons, buggies, and saddle horses began to arrive shortly before eight o'clock. I was already in the classroom and had a big pot of water heating for making the coffee. Coffee tonight would be free, as was the milk for the children. All else would be paid for and the money would go into the Pastachuck fund.

The schoolroom began to fill with excited children and chattering grown-ups. The attendance was going to be good and the little schoolroom was going to be crowded. Already some of the men were opening windows. *How good of these people to care and do something about the need of a family in their community. Bless our efforts, Lord,* I prayed silently.

I had prepared carefully for the evening, putting on one of my favorite gowns. I knew that I was a bit overdressed for this informal occasion, but somehow I thought that folks would expect it of me. I had arranged my hair with fastidious curls, which I heaped mostly on the top of my head, carefully letting one or two hang down on one side. My appearance was not unnoticed by the cluster of single fellows near the door, who were ogling, guffawing, and slapping one another on the back.

The Delaneys arrived. Mr. Delaney found his mother a chair and took the coats of his womenfolk to pile on a corner table with those of their neighbors'; we had long ago run out of coat hooks. The younger Mrs. Delaney reached a hand up to her hair, then smoothed her already smooth skirt. Her back was to me, so I couldn't see her face. I wanted to look at her—and I didn't, both at the same time. She stood chatting with neighbors, a slim, dark-haired young woman, attractively attired. I found myself noting that her dress was not nearly as pretty as mine and immediately rebuked myself for my cattiness.

When Mr. Delaney had gotten the womenfolk settled, he moved off to chat with some of the neighborhood men. The crowd around Mrs. Delaney thinned somewhat and she took a chair. I saw her clearly then. Dark eyes sparkled under long, dark lashes. She had a straight, rather small nose. Her cheeks were flushed with excitement and full rosy lips parted slightly as she smiled easily at those she greeted. She was more than just attractive.

I turned back to my duties but had hardly organized my thoughts before I felt a tug on my hand.

"Miss Thatcher, my mom wants to meet you." It was Phillip.

For a moment near-panic seized me, but I knew that I was being foolish. It was inevitable that I meet this woman, and it may as well be now. I prepared my nicest smile and let Phillip lead me toward her.

As we approached, her eyes lit up, and she stood to her feet.

"Miss Thatcher," she said warmly, extending her hand, "I'm so happy to meet you at last. I'm Lydia Delaney. I've heard so many nice things about you."

She was so sincere, so open and friendly that I responded to her immediately.

"Thank you," I said; "it's nice to meet Phillip's mother." I meant those words.

She looked me over appreciatively. "No wonder Phillip was happy to stay after school."

I smiled. Phillip still held my hand, and he beamed up at me. I put my arm around his shoulders and gave him a squeeze. I'm sure that she could see how I felt about Phillip. I spoke then to the elder Mrs. Delaney; she took my hand in both of hers and greeted me.

"I'm so sorry," said Lydia, "that we haven't yet had you over, but things have been so unsettled at our house. We have been off to Calgary most weekends and, well, we hope that things will soon change so we can return to normal living."

Called away by one of my students, I had to excuse myself. I walked away with the feeling of Lydia Delaney's warm, brown eyes upon me.

The evening progressed well. I was kept busy circulating among the students and helping them in any way that I could with their booths. Every now and then a whispered report was given to me of how many pennies had been collected at a certain station. The students were excited about their achievements.

Activity at the booths began slowing down as the people started to think of the lunch boxes. We cleared some more room for chairs and benches by putting aside the games from the booths and taking down some of the dividers strung on the wires. Then Mr. Dickerson took his place at the front.

Anna Peterson and Mrs. Blake were not the only women who had packed for extra mouths. Many of the boxes were enormous. As the bidding began, it became apparent that Mrs. Blake was not the only woman who had informed her spouse what to look for. Without exception, husband and wife got together and spread out their goodies for themselves and their offspring.

I watched with interest and amusement as Mr. Delaney prompted Phillip in the bidding for his mother's basket. Phillip felt very grown-up as he shouted his bid, and when he had finally been successful in his purchase, Mr. Delaney counted out the money for him to pay the auctioneer's clerk himself.

The older girls had their own baskets, and the older boys, with dimes, quarters, red faces, and much teasing, lined up to make their bids.

My basket was the last one to be held up. I scolded myself for my flushed cheeks and wished with all of my heart that I had begged off from participating. It was apparently common knowledge about whose basket was being offered, for the young men moved in from beside the door, and the bidding opened vigorously. The color in my cheeks deepened with each bid; I kept my eyes averted and pretended to be very busy serving coffee. The teasing and joking did not escape me; but it was a few moments before I realized that Mr. Delaney was among the bidders. This knowledge upset me so that I could not stop my hand from shaking as I poured coffee.

Why would he do that? *Why?* There sat his wife and his mother—right before his eyes, and here he was . . . I choked on the humiliation for us all. A new thought struck me. Perhaps his mother had fixed a box, and he supposed this to be it. I glanced around the room and could see that such wasn't the case, for there sat the two Mrs. Delaneys and Phillip sharing a chat with the Blakes as they ate their respective lunches. Lydia Delaney chatted gaily with Mrs. Blake, stopping occasionally to smile at the antics of the bidders.

How can she? I thought. *How can she? She must be humiliated nearly to death. How can she endure it so calmly? Is she used to such behavior? Doesn't it bother her when her husband publicly deserts her?*

She certainly appeared unperturbed by it all. In fact, one could even have accused her of enjoying it. Was it just a cover-up? My anger boiled hotter with each bid placed by Mr. Delaney.

There was much laughter, shouted comments, and jockeying for position as the bids climbed. Finally only Bill Laverly and Mr. Delaney remained as bidders. I had never expected to find myself championing the grinning Bill Laverly, but I did so now, hoping with all my heart that he would outbid the other man. At a bid from Mr. Delaney, Bill went down on both knees and began to empty all of his pockets, spreading out all of his bills and change, even offering the auctioneer chewing tobacco and a pocket knife. There was much knee-slapping, joking, and clapping by the appreciative crowd. It was obvious that Bill could go no higher. He implored some of his buddies for a loan, and the bidding continued. But it was Mr. Delaney who was finally handed the basket as he paid the clerk.

I was furious, not just for my sake—but for *hers.*

I knew that I was expected to leave my coffee-pouring and go share lunch with the man who had purchased my basket, but I couldn't—and I wouldn't.

I turned and said in a loud, though somewhat unsteady, voice, hoping that the smile I was trying so hard to produce actually showed on my face, "Mr. Delaney has just purchased a bigger bargain than he realizes. Because my duties will be keeping me busy, he gets to eat all of the lunch himself."

Laughter followed my announcement, along with hoots from the young men who had lost out in the bidding. I turned back to the pot of coffee, not daring to look at Mr. Delaney again. *And I hope he chokes on it,* I thought angrily. Three women rushed with offers to take over my job so that I could sit down and enjoy my lunch. I turned them all aside—firmly, and I hoped, courteously. I later noticed Mr. Delaney sharing his lunch with some good-natured chatter with Andy Pastachuck.

As the evening drew to a close, the money was gathered and counted. We placed it all in a big tin can and had Mr. Laverly, our school-board chairman, present it to the Pastachucks. They accepted it with broken English and tear-filled eyes. They planned to leave soon for Calgary and a doctor, and would send word back as soon as they had a report. Teresa was to stay with the Blakes during their absence, and the Thebeaus had volunteered to care for their farm chores.

It didn't seem quite fitting to simply pass them the money and send them on their way, so I stepped forward hesitantly. First I thanked all of those who had come and participated so wholeheartedly. Our total earnings, including donations from neighbors, came to $195.64. A cheer went up when the sum was announced.

"We all have learned to love Andy," I continued. "Our thoughts and prayers will be with him and his parents, and as a token of our prayers and concern, I would like to ask Mr. Dickerson, our auctioneer of the evening, to lead us in prayer on Andy's behalf."

A silence fell over the room. Eyes filled with tears, heads bowed, and calloused hands reached up to sweep hats aside.

Mr. Dickerson stepped to the center of the room and cleared his throat. His simple and sincere prayer was followed by many whispered "Amens."

Our evening together had ended. Folks crowded around me shaking my hand, saying kind words and thanking me for my efforts toward the success of the evening. I felt very much at one with these gentle, warmhearted people.

The Pastachucks were the last to go. Mr. Pastachuck offered his hand and shook mine firmly. His wife could only smile through tears, unable to speak. But Andy looked at me with shining eyes, as though to herald a personal triumph on my behalf. "It was fun," he enthused. "You did good, Teacher, real good!"

I reached down and pulled him close, holding him for a long time; his thin little arms were wrapped tightly about my neck. When I released him, I was crying. Andy reached up and, without a word, brushed the tears from my cheek. Then he turned and walked out into the night.

TWENTY-SIX

Andy

Midweek, word came from Calgary. As we had feared, Andy's condition was serious. The old injury had flared up. A tumor had formed, causing pressure on the brain. The doctor suspected that bone chips were responsible, and he decided that surgery was imperative as soon as possible.

The whole class wrote notes to Andy to send with Mrs. Blake and Teresa to the hospital. The outcome of the pending surgery was sufficiently doubtful that Teresa was being taken to Calgary to see her brother before his operation.

I wrote a note, too. It was short and simply worded so that Andy would have no trouble understanding it when it was read to him. I said that we were all very busy at school; that we thought of him and prayed for him daily in our opening prayer; that we missed him and would be so glad when he would be well and able to be back with us.

But Andy did not return. He died during surgery in the Calgary hospital. We were told that even the nurses who attended him wept when the small boy lost his battle for life.

It was a Wednesday afternoon when we all gathered at the schoolhouse for Andy's short funeral service. Mr. Dickerson read the scripture, and a visiting priest gave the last rites. We then left for the little cemetery on the hill.

Many of my pupils were crying as we filed from the schoolroom. Else Peterson and Mindy Blake clung to each of my hands. My eyes were overflowing, but I was able to keep the sobs from shaking me.

It was a short distance to the cemetery so we walked to it, the little procession, with the small pine casket at its head, stirring up little pillowy swirls of dust. The day was bright, the autumn sun glistening in a tranquil sky. A few clouds skittered across the blueness. The leaves still clinging to the trees were in full dress, but many others lay scattered on the ground, rustling at each stirring of the breeze.

Else broke our silence.

"Andy would have liked this day," she whispered, looking up at its brightness; and I knew that she was right. I could imagine the gentle little boy with his shining eyes cheering this day on.

"You did good," he would exclaim to the beautiful morning. "You did good."

I cried then, the great sobs shaking my whole body. I remembered the last time that I had wept, and how the little boy in my embrace had reached up awkwardly, and yet tenderly, to brush away my tears. "You did good, Teacher," he had whispered. And now that small boy had passed beyond—so young to journey on alone. But then I remembered that he hadn't traveled alone—not one step of the way, for as soon as the loving hands had released him here, another Hand had reached out to gently take him. I tried to visualize him entering that new Land, the excitement and eagerness shining forth on his face, the cheers raising from the shrill little voice. There would be no pain twisting his face now, no need to hold his head and rock back and forth. Joy and happiness would surround him. I could almost hear his words as he looked at the glories of heaven and gave the Father his jubilant ovation—"You did good, God; You did real good!"

TWENTY-SEVEN
School Break

We decided to close school for the rest of that week. All of the students were deeply affected by the loss of Andy, and Mr. Laverly thought that it would do us all good to have a few days of rest. I agreed. I suddenly felt very tired. I would go to visit Jon and his family.

That afternoon, I packed a few things in a small suitcase and asked for a ride to town. Mr. Mattoch, who had a light buggy with spring seats, was my driver. The trip was much more comfortable and took considerably less time than had the previous wagon transportation.

The train did not leave for Calgary until the next morning, so I took a room in the hotel and spent a miserable, lonely night there. The next morning I spent some time shopping until the train came. I didn't see anything which attracted me, but perhaps it was my mood rather than the lack of merchandise.

Finally I was Calgary bound; but the train did not seem to be nearly as eager to reach Calgary as I was. The first thing I did upon my arrival was to telephone Jon's home. Mary answered, and her excitement at hearing my voice went a long way toward cheering me. Jon arrived to pick me up at the station before I had time to properly get myself in order. He had just purchased a new Buick and was anxious to show it off. Not many autos had as yet made their way onto the Calgary streets, and those who did use the new means of conveyance seemed to consider it a daily challenge to try and outdo one another both in model and speed.

When we pulled up in front of Jon's house, the entire family was waiting to welcome me. Even little William gave his aunt a big hug. I'm afraid that I clung to the children longer than I should have, my sorrow still very fresh in my mind and heart.

One could not nurse sadness for long in Jonathan's home. The children's shouts of excitement gave me little time to think about the loss of Andy. They promptly showed me everything that they had attained or obtained since I had left them. William presented a new bow and arrow, and Sarah read to me from her first primer; but Kathleen wouldn't even leave my side long enough to produce her new dress or her doll.

They all shared in presenting to me the much-grown Elizabeth and her latest accomplishments. She could smile, she could coo, and once she even giggled. The little sweetheart warmed up to me immediately and allowed me to hold and cuddle her.

I did not need to return to Pine Springs until the following Monday. The train ran north on Monday, Wednesday and Friday; and south on Tuesday, Thursday and Saturday; so the days that Mr. Laverly had set aside for this school break were planned accordingly. The long weekend that stretched before me seemed nicely adequate for my visit, but I knew that the days would go all too quickly.

On Saturday, Kathleen danced into my room before my eyes were even properly open. "Dee is coming! Dee is coming!" she cried with glee.

I smiled at her sleepily, thinking, *Who is Dee?* Then I recalled her long-ago declaration of, "When I grow up, I'm gonna marry Dee." I yawned and rolled over to look at her. My thoughts changed to, So, *I am to meet Kathleen's marvelous Dee, the thirtyish bachelor who is a dear—and determined to stay single.*

He sounded harmless enough to me.

"When is Dee coming?" I asked as Kathleen twirled about my room.

"Tonight—for dinner. Did you meet him yet?"

"No, not yet," I answered rather casually.

"Did you know that I'm gonna marry him when I grow up?" she asked, not a bit put off by my nonchalance.

"I remember that you told me," I answered her.

She was soon gone again, off to share her good news with her baby sister—who would be even less impressed than I had been.

As the day wore on, the anticipation for the evening dinner party grew. It was obvious that the whole family regarded Dee highly and were pleased that he was coming.

I dressed carefully for dinner that night, not because of the unknown Dee but simply because it felt good to soak in a warm bath and then spend a little more time and effort than usual on how I looked. It seemed to be such a long time since our box social and I had reason to dress up. Kathleen came in to offer suggestions and coaxed me to wear the green velvet. It was still hanging in the guest room closet, a last-minute decision when I had left for Pine Springs. "I will never need a fussy thing like that in a country school," I had impulsively declared. "Mary, do you mind if I just leave it hanging here?" Mary agreed, so I had unwrapped it from its tissues and left it hanging in the spare bedroom. Now it shimmered in the light and caught Kathleen's eye. I gave in to her pleading. She helped me with my buttons, and I retied her hair ribbon so that we could state that we had helped one another to prepare for dinner.

She skipped out as I put the finishing touches on my hair, but she was soon back.

"Dee is here!" she exclaimed excitedly. "Hurry—hurry!"

"I'm coming, dear," I laughed. She grabbed my hand, eager to drag me off to meet her Dee. I did hope that he wasn't another Mr. Higgins, but I quickly discarded that idea. I gave Kathleen credit for better judgment than that.

"Nanna is here, too," she informed me as she led me through the hallway and down the stairs.

"Nanna?"

"Yes, Nanna. Mamma's grannie. Nanna Smith."

"Oh," I said in surprise. "I didn't know that Nanna was coming."

"Mamma didn't know, either," Kathleen laughed. "Mamma never knows. Nanna just comes—she likes surprises."

"Oh, I see—like your Aunt Beth did, I guess. She just popped in."

Kathleen laughed merrily at that.

"You *couldn't* tell us," she said, having heard the explanation I gave to Mary, "but Nanna could. She lives just over by the river. She could have telephoned or anything—but she doesn't. She just comes. She likes surprises. We like it, too. It's fun."

A few minutes later I was meeting Nanna, an older woman with a sparkle in her eyes. I could easily imagine that she indeed liked surprises. I had always felt that I liked surprises myself—until the one I received in the next few minutes.

Kathleen had left me with Nanna and had run to find her Dee so that I might have the pleasure of making his acquaintance. I stood chatting, my back to the door, until Kathleen called out merrily, "Here's Dee, Aunt Beth."

I turned slowly around and found myself looking into the face of Mr. Wynn Delaney.

My face must have blanched.

I could not find my voice; I could only stare. My mind groped for an answer; how could this dreadful mix-up ever have taken place? For a moment I thought that I read concern in his eyes, and I wondered if he feared that I might divulge something he would rather have left secret.

The color seemed to be returning to my face—in overabundance, I feared; but I felt that perhaps I could move again.

I saw Mr. Delaney advance a step and place an arm around Kathleen's shoulder. The flash of concern had left his eyes, and a teasing smile replaced it.

"Your Aunt Beth and I have already met, Moppet."

I remained dumb. "You're—?

"Dee—" he finished for me. "William's two-year-old version of 'Delaney'! All of these children have called me that."

"I see. . . ."

I didn't really. The pieces of this strange puzzle didn't fit together at all. Something was all wrong here.

"Mr.—De—Delaney," I stammered, knowing even as I spoke that what I was asking was foolish indeed, "do you happen to have a twin?"

He seemed about to laugh at that, and then realized that my question had been an honest one. He shook his head, then looked at me with renewed concern. My bewildered eyes and flushed face must have made him think that something was wrong with me, for he gently took my arm and led me to a nearby chair.

"Are you all right?" he asked in a low voice.

I assured him shakily that I was just fine.

His inbred courtesy prompted him to turn then to speak with Nanna, whom he seemed to know very well.

I sat numbly, listening to the hum of voices about me. Mr. Delaney and Nanna chatted like old friends. Suddenly Kathleen, who had been left out of the conversation for what she felt was too long, announced, "Did you know I'm gonna marry Dee, Nanna?"

The conversation stopped. Dee reached for Kathleen and seated her beside him on the lounge where he sat.

"What's this, Moppet?"

"I'm gonna *marry* you," she said, pointing a finger at his broad chest. "I'm gonna marry you when I grow up. Right?"

"I don't suppose so." He spoke very slowly, carefully. "You see, just because one likes someone very much doesn't always mean that they will get married. People can still be very special to one another—the best friends in the whole world—and not marry."

Kathleen's face began to cloud.

"Take you now," Mr. Delaney hurried on, "you love your daddy—very much—but you don't need to marry him to share that love, do you?"

Kathleen slowly shook her head.

"And you love your mamma, and Nanna, and Baby Elizabeth, and your Aunt Beth and your Teddy—but you aren't going to marry *them* either, are you?"

Kathleen brightened at the twinkle in his eyes, seeing the fun that he was having.

He continued, "Well, that's like us. We are very special to one another, but we don't need to marry each other to stay special."

Kathleen nodded. Dee had been quite convincing.

Mary called, and Kathleen bounced down from the lounge, her recently troubled eyes again shining, and ran from the room.

"You could have humored her a bit," scolded Nanna.

"How?"

"Well, you could have said, 'Someday—sure, someday.'"

"But it won't be 'someday.'"

"Yes, *we* know that—and Kathleen would know it too, as she grew older."

"But if she didn't?"

"She's only a child."

"A child who will grow up. Yet she will still be a child for many years to come. What would happen, Nanna, if I found someone else to marry before she discovered the truth on her own?"

"You—marry?" Nanna laughed.

Mr. Delaney smiled slowly as though enjoying his own joke.

"Or, what if she didn't discover the truth on her own and went into womanhood expecting this *old* man to marry her?"

Nanna shrugged and said teasingly, "Maybe the day will come when you'll be glad to accept her proposal."

Mr. Delaney became serious then. "If ever anyone deserves the truth, Nanna," he said, "a child does. They can accept things, even hurtful things, if they are dealt with honestly, in love. I hope that I'm never guilty of telling a falsehood to a trusting child."

His words hung about my head, making me angry. How could he say these things—he who was living a horrible lie. I excused myself from the room and headed for my bedroom. I feared that I was going to be sick.

Mary found me a few minutes later.

"Dee was worried about you, Beth. Is something wrong?"

Everything is wrong, I wanted to scream—*Everything.* Instead I said, "Mary, didn't you tell me that Wynn Delaney—Dee—whoever, is unmarried?"

"Yes."

"And didn't you say that he—he wanted to *stay* that way?"

She nodded.

"Well, maybe—" I said, blanching white again, "maybe, the reason that he hasn't taken a Calgary wife is that *he already has one.*"

"Wynn?" Mary used his given name.

"Yes, Wynn."

"That's impossible. We've know Wynn—"

"Well, apparently you don't know him very well."

"Elizabeth, we know—"

"He *has* a wife—and a son. I've met them."

"You've what?"

"His son, Phillip, is my student."

"Phillip?"

"Yes, Phillip, and I've—"

"Elizabeth, Phillip is Lydia and Phillip's child."

"Whose?"

"Lydia and—"

"Is she divorced?"

"Lydia?" Mary's voice was incredulous.

"She lives with *Wynn,*" I insisted.

"Wynn is the senior Phillip's brother."

"And where is this—this other Phillip?"

"Here—in the hospital. That's why Wynn is in Calgary so often. Lydia and Phillip, Jr. are here now too, staying with her parents."

My knees felt weak. I groped behind me for the bed and sat down.

"Beth—are you all right?" Mary asked anxiously.

I honestly didn't know. My head was whirling and my stomach was in knots.

After a long silence, I whispered, "Mary, are you *sure?*"

"I'm sure—*very* sure."

Parts of the crazy puzzle began to slip into place. Lydia—her friendliness—her statement that "everything has been so upset"—

her ability to laugh and enjoy the spectacle of the battle for my box at the social.

"Oh, Mary," I moaned, but I could say no more. I buried my face in my hands and thought of the times when I had been rude—inexcusably so, I was now discovering—to Wynn Delaney. How could I ever make him understand? How could I ever make things right?

"They have good news," Mary continued brightly. "Phillip can go home on Monday. I talked to Lydia today, and she is wild with excitement."

"I'm—I'm sure—I'm sure she is," I stammered.

"I must go, Beth. Are you sure you're okay?"

I managed a weak smile. "Sure—I'm fine—just fine. Just give me a minute or two and I'll be right down. I guess things just caught up with me all of a sudden. Don't worry. I'm all right."

Mary left, and I tried hard to find some composure. My heart thumped so hard I could almost hear it.

Wynn Delaney was not a married man. He was not Lydia's husband. He was not *anyone's* husband. And so many times, when he had made some small gesture of kindness, I had coldly rebuffed him. How would I ever explain my foolishness? What must he think of me? Now I *knew* that I was going to be sick.

TWENTY-EIGHT

Dee

I did appear for dinner. I must have still been pale, and I felt that my smile looked a little weak; but in the midst of the chatter and laughter around the table, I hoped that it wasn't noticed. I was quiet during the meal, but I never had done a lot of talking, and I was able to respond when I was spoken to.

Kathleen had requested that she sit between *her* Dee and *her* Aunt Beth, and on this occasion her mother saw no harm in humoring her; after all, she had just been "jilted" by the man whom she had planned to marry. Dee fussed over her, perhaps in an effort to show her that he still cared about her even though the wedding was "off." Kathleen did not act as one forsaken and forgotten. Her little tongue was constantly going, telling Dee of her new doll—"show ya right after dinner"; her new green dress—"almost the color of Aunt Beth's"; what she did while Sarah was at school—"helped Mamma"; and how much Baby Elizabeth liked her.

Occasionally Kathleen would say, "Isn't that right, Aunt Beth?" And I would be obliged to enter into their conversation.

I was glad for the seating arrangement. At least I did not have to sit opposite Wynn Delaney—Kathleen's Dee—where I would have to look at him once in a while throughout the meal. Those sensitive eyes might look right through me and see my tumbled emotions.

When Jonathan decided that there had been enough children's chatter, he excused them from the table to go to their rooms for a bit of play before bedtime.

The grown-ups then had a quieter conversation over second cups of coffee. I had preferred the din of the children, for with their leaving attention suddenly focused uncomfortably on me. Jon and Mary plied me with questions about my school, my pupils, my neighbors, and my little teacherage. Because I loved them all so much, I imagine that love showed in my eyes and voice, in spite of the way I was feeling.

"Elizabeth must be very tired," Wynn interjected after a time, and I looked at him in surprise. For one thing, I had never heard him call me "Elizabeth" before.

"She's been working very hard with her students," he elaborated, "and then she took on the extra load of organizing a money-raising social for a local family in need."

I had already told Jon and Mary about Andy, and the eyes around the table softened at the mention of the fund-raising effort.

I swallowed hard. I still found my heart hurting at the mention of the dear little fellow.

"The work wasn't too much," I hurried to explain. "If things had turned out differently—"

Wynn reached across the empty chair that separated us and gave my hand a sympathetic squeeze. Shocked, I looked up quickly to catch the expression in the eyes around the table. But no one looked surprised. I presumed they understood such gestures better than I did—and they also knew the man better than I. Mary quickly took charge of the situation. I think that she was a little afraid that talking of Andy would have me weeping again.

"I have four children to care for," she announced with a smile. "Jon, dear, why don't you move our guests to a more comfortable setting, and I'll join you in a few minutes."

"I must go, my dear," Nanna said, rising. "This has been lovely, and I so much enjoy sharing dinner with you and your children. It's much better than sitting up to a table alone." She gave a mock shiver. Mary stopped to kiss her on the cheek.

"We love to have you. You just come over whenever you wish."

"Oh, I do—I do," she said with a twinkle.

Jon took Nanna home. We all said appropriate things as we bid her good-bye, and then Mary hurried upstairs to put the children to bed.

The moment that I had dreaded had come. I knew that Wynn deserved an explanation for my rudeness in days past, but I didn't know quite how to approach the subject.

Wynn and I were sent to the front parlor and each given another cup of coffee—which I neither wanted nor needed, but at least the cup gave me something to do with my nervous hands. I knew that Jon would soon be back to join us, so I decided I dared not fill in the time with small talk.

"I'm afraid that I owe you an explanation," I began in a rather quavering voice as soon as we were seated before the fire.

He had been watching the flames, but he turned to look at me. I didn't know if it was my words or my voice that gave away the fact that what I had to say was important.

His eyes held a question but he did not speak, so I went on.

"You see, I thought—that is, I understood, that—that you were Phillip's father."

His jaw dropped with astonishment.

"You thought that I—that I—that my brother's wife was raising my child?"

"I didn't know that you had a brother."

"You thought that—that *what*?"

"I thought that Lydia was *your* wife."

"But how. . . ?" He shook his head in disbelief, then held up a hand as though to stop me from proceeding too quickly. Finally he spoke again. "Lydia is a sweet, lovely woman—but my brother Phillip is the fortunate man."

"I know that *now.* Mary told me."

He stood up and paced a few steps, then stood gazing into the fire. When he swiveled to face me, his face was still filled with puzzlement.

"You thought that I—was a married man?"

"Yes."

He again shook his head, then stood thoughtfully looking into the fire. Finally he turned toward me.

"Where did you ever get such an idea?" His tone was not accusing, merely baffled. But I was on the defensive now. Surely it wasn't all stupidity on my part. Tears were stinging my eyelids. I stood to my feet.

"I got the idea," I said, with deliberate emphasis, "because *you* were living in the same house as Lydia, *you* came to school to see me about young Phillip, *you* asked me for his homework, *you* spoke of 'his mother and I,' and *you* shared the same last name—and *nobody* ever mentioned to me that there was such a person as Phillip, Sr."

My voice had become quite loud by the time I had finished my speech. The astonished look left his face as he followed my reasoning; a look of frustration took its place.

"I see . . ." he said a little lamely when I had finished, and he turned to the flames again.

I sat back down. My hands were trembling. Carefully I set my cup and saucer on the small table beside my chair.

"I see," he said again, and turned back to me. "So, figuratively speaking, you tossed your box lunch back in my face?" Again, his openness and honesty took the sting out of the words.

I couldn't speak. I couldn't even look up. I just sat there twisting my handkerchief slowly around a finger and feeling the color rising into my face. Suddenly I heard a soft chuckle. I looked up quickly then, wondering why his sudden change of mood.

"It's rather funny, isn't it?" His eyes held their usual good humor, and he chuckled again. "Here I spend ten dollars and sixty-five cents so that I can sit with the pretty schoolteacher; and, instead, I eat alone because she thinks—"

"You paid *ten dollars and sixty-five cents?* For a box lunch?"

He laughed as he nodded sheepishly, like a schoolboy.

"But that's—that's ridiculous! All of the baskets were going for one or two—"

"Not that one."

Now my face was hot with embarrassment. That evening I had

not paid attention to the price that my basket had brought.

"It was a good cause," he assured me seriously, "so I do not begrudge the ten-sixty-five."

I remembered little Andy again. It *had* been a good cause. . . .

"And," he said, this time in false lament, "it could have been a good *buy* as well."

"I'm—I'm sorry. Truly, I—I—"

"So am I, Miss Thatcher." His eyes fixed on mine for an instant, then he turned back to the fire.

The few seconds of awkward silence that followed seemed far longer.

"Actually," he ventured, "perhaps it was all for the best." He stepped back from the fire and took the seat opposite me, putting down his now-empty cup.

"The *best?"* I questioned, not understanding him.

"I'm afraid I was beginning to think like a farmer."

"And there is something *wrong* with thinking like a farmer?"

He smiled. "Not for a farmer."

"And—you're not a farmer?"

"I?"

I nodded.

"No, not I."

"But you—"

"I was given a special leave so that I could give Phillip a hand—to take off his crop. I was raised on the farm, so at least I know what to do and when to do it. I even enjoyed it—for a change. Once or twice, I even wished that I had stayed on the farm myself. A farmer is, after all, his own boss—to the extent that the elements will allow him, while . . ." He paused and shrugged. "But Phillip will soon be back to again take charge of his farm—and his son—*and* his wife."

He was teasing, and I once more felt my face flush.

I wanted to ask what he now would do, where his work would take him, but I didn't. Instead, I went to the window and looked out on the quiet evening. I was just in time to see Jon return from taking Nanna home.

"I think that I will go say good-night to the children," I said and gathered up the coffee cups to take them to the kitchen.

I felt his eyes upon me as I left the room. It was rather impolite of me to desert him, but Jon would soon be in to keep him company.

TWENTY-NINE

Return to School

We saw Wynn, Lydia, and Phillip, Jr. at church the next morning, but we had little opportunity to chat. I was glad about that. I still had some sorting out to do.

That afternoon, Mary and I had some time alone; she directed the conversation to Wynn.

"So," she said directly, "what do you think of our Dee—now that you've allowed him his rightful single status?" She laughed as she said it, and I tried to laugh with her, but I flushed too.

"He's—he's a very nice man." The words sounded silly, but I couldn't think of anything else that I felt was appropriate to say.

"He's more than nice," Mary said with enthusiasm. "He's—very special. I had even dared to hope—" She restrained herself, and looked at me quickly as though to see if I had caught on to what she had been about to say. Changing her mind, she said, "Just wish he weren't so stubborn."

"Stubborn?"

"Well, not about everything, but he's got this crazy notion that marriage and his work do not go together."

"Oh?" I was hoping she would understand that as a question.

"He's determined—absolutely determined—that he will *never* ask a woman to share his life with him. He says that other men can run their lives in this order: God, wife, work; but his has to be God, work, wife, and he won't ask a woman to take the lesser position."

"My, my," I said, trying to sound casual and even a bit sarcastic, "he must be a *very* special man."

"No, no. *He* doesn't think he's special. He just thinks that his *job* is. He's totally dedicated to it—but then, of course, it does take him into some rather primitive settings. He has already spent time up north, and I'm sure he will again. And he says that he won't ask a woman to share that. I guess it's rather tough—"

"But if a woman really loved a man," I interrupted, "surely she wouldn't mind . . . Doesn't he know there is such a thing as love—real love—and if a woman—"

"Little Beth," Mary said, her eyes twinkling, "maybe you'll have to show him."

"Now wait a minute . . ." I started, blushing to my roots. Mary laughed outright.

"I really don't think that he would be such a difficult pupil; and I have heard that you're a *good* teacher," she teased.

Though blushing and tongue-tied, I still refused to be baited.

"So—" I began, trying to gain control of the conversation—and myself, "what is this special, oh-so-important, impossible-to-live-with job?"

Mary became serious. "You don't know what Wynn does?"

"No. Why should I know?"

"He's a Mountie."

"What?"

"A North West Mounted Policeman."

"I know what a Mountie is. I'm just surprised. I never thought . . ."

Then, as if I finally had found the lever to release the nervous tension of the previous twenty-four hours, I burst out in laughter. "Julie would swoon," I gasped out.

"What?"

"Oh, nothing." I was starting to recover from my laughing.

Baby Elizabeth cried, and Mary rushed off to look after her. I was left alone with my churning thoughts and emotions.

I remembered the words, ". . . I was beginning to think like a farmer," and I thought that I now understood what Wynn had meant—at least a bit. A farmer certainly didn't need to worry about his work conflicting with the taking of a wife.

On Monday morning I wanted to spend time in the local library to search out some information I needed in my teaching; I asked Jon if he would drive me downtown well before train time. So he delivered me to the station where we purchased my ticket and left my suitcase with the clerk. I bid Jon good-bye, trying hard to explain just how much the weekend had meant to me. I now felt ready to return to my classroom.

I walked the short distance to the library and began to browse through the titles. It was a small library so I had not bothered asking for help but went looking on my own. My eyes caught a rather unusual title, *The Origin and Meaning of Names.* I pulled it from the shelf and flipped through the pages. I found "Elizabeth." It was Hebrew, the book said, and meant "consecrated to God." The meaning pleased me. It was nice to belong to Him.

I cast a quick look around to see if anyone was near, then turned quickly to the W's. I didn't expect to find Wynn, but I did. "Old Welsh," it said—"fair one." I closed the book quickly and tucked the small bit of information away. I agreed with the book. I then thought of Mary's teasing—that *I* should try to change Wynn's mind about marriage. Against my will, the idea popped into my mind, *I'd like to—I'd really LIKE to.* With a smile I thought that I should have taken lessons in winsomeness from Julie. I had no idea how to go about changing a man's mind—especially regarding marriage. I jolted myself from my reverie and set about searching for the information I needed for teaching.

Boarding the train in plenty of time, I selected my seat. It appeared that the coach would not be very full. I settled myself for a long, tedious journey as we pulled away from the depot. This time I was prepared—I had brought along a book to read. Perhaps the stopping and unloading, loading and shuffling, would not bother me quite so much if I kept my mind occupied.

I couldn't concentrate on my book. I found myself staring out of the window watching the slowly passing landscape and the bustle of activity in the small towns where we stopped to exchange passengers and cargo. As we pulled out of Red Deer, I decided to take a walk through the coach and stretch my legs.

When I stood up and looked down the car, I discovered that I had been sharing the car with the Delaneys. I attempted to quietly sit back down before I was spotted, but Lydia noticed me. She waved and I returned her greeting, and then she beckoned me to come and join them. I didn't see how I could politely refuse. Wynn rose to his feet as I approached them, and he motioned for me to take his seat beside Phillip, Jr., facing Lydia and Phillip, Sr. I had not met the elder Phillip before. It would have been easy to tell that he and Wynn were brothers, even though Phillip was pale from his hospital stay and was shorter and fairer than Wynn. Lydia was beside herself with joy; it was plain to see that she had missed her husband terribly, and I imagined the strain it must have been on her. No wonder there had been so many weekend trips to Calgary. It seemed strange to me that Phillip had never mentioned his father, but perhaps that was the way the small boy had determined to handle his anxiety. In fact, I had never heard him refer to his Uncle Wynn either, though he certainly seemed to think highly of him.

"Mother is waiting at home," Lydia confided. "She can hardly wait for Phil to get home so that she can fatten him up! I can imagine that she's been cooking for two days straight."

"I'm willing," her husband said. "I am so weary of hospital cooking that I'll be happy to have Mother fuss for a while. I see that she's managed to put a few pounds on Wynn—though I'm sure that it wasn't as many as she would have liked."

"That was a difficult assignment," Lydia jested. "Wynn worked it off as quickly as Mother cooked it on."

Young Phillip decided to take his new *Animals of the World* picture book to the seat across the aisle. I then moved over so that Wynn might sit down again.

Although Phil seemed to have the same sense of humor as his brother, he didn't possess quite the same unruffled confidence. *Perhaps it is because Phillip has been ill,* I reasoned. But even beyond that, there was something about Wynn that set him apart. *Maybe being a member of the Mounted Police has given him assurance,* I further told myself—but that didn't seem to be the whole answer either. I finally decided that it was just "Wynn." That was why he took his work so seriously and why he was capable of such dedication to his difficult job. I was convinced that he must be a very efficient member of the Force.

I said that I was so glad Phil was now able to rejoin his family.

"I'm sure that Wynn, also, is glad to see me finally make it," said Phil. "I think that he may be a bit tired of riding the binder and milking the cows."

"Soft touch!" was Wynn's rejoinder.

"Now he's going to tell me that he'll be glad to get back to some *real* work," Phil predicted.

"Right," teased Wynn, "I was getting—"

"Don't say it." Phil held up his hand. "Soft or not, we couldn't have made it without you."

"You'll need a few months to regain your strength, but I guess you'll get it back during the winter. It'll be five months before you'll need to put your hand to the plow."

"I'm afraid that I'm going to have a tough job holding him down," said Lydia.

"Young Thebeau is good with stock. There's no excuse for Phil to get out there," Wynn assured her.

The Delaneys continued discussing future plans, and I realized that Wynn had no thought of staying on at the farm once Phil was home again. I wondered where he was going and if I'd ever see him again. But I was afraid to ask.

I noticed Lydia holding Phil's hand tightly. She looked as if she were afraid to let go, lest he leave her again. I could imagine how many things they had to talk about. I stood up.

"I must get back to my seat," I said. "I need to gather my things together."

Wynn stood and moved aside so that I could pass him. The train gave a sudden lurch, and I nearly lost my balance. His arm was quick to steady me. I hurriedly righted myself by grabbing the back of a seat and withdrew from him. This contact, however short and unplanned, had unnerved me.

I had gathered my few belongings together in short order and knew by the landmarks that we still had some minutes left before arrival. I picked up my book and stared at the pages, but I didn't read. I heard a stirring and looked up in time to see Wynn lower himself in the seat opposite me.

"May I?"

"Certainly."

"I wondered if you had arranged for a way home."

"I—not really. I guess when I left I wasn't thinking that far ahead."

"Fine. Then you can ride with us."

"I—thank you."

"You don't mind?"

"No, of course not. That is, if *you* don't mind."

"Then it's settled."

He was about to go but I detained him. "Mr. Delaney," I said. I had never called him by his first name, though I thought of him as "Wynn." "I know that I tried to explain about the box social, but I didn't say how—how sorry I am for publicly embarrassing you."

"Embarrassing me?"

"Yes. Even though I thought that you were married, your neighbors—they knew that you weren't, and they had no idea that I thought—what I did—and—"

"Would it have made a difference?" His tone was forthright. "Would you have *found* time to share your lunch if you had known the truth?"

"Of course."

He considered that for a moment.

I started, "Why else would I—"

"Miss Thatcher," he said and he grinned at me—that slow, teasing grin, "I am not so conceited as to believe that a young lady such as yourself, cultured and refined, would jump at the chance of sharing a lunch with the likes of me—untamed and unpolished—under any circumstances. You were quite within your rights to turn me down—for whatever your reason—no questions asked."

I gasped.

"But—but I *wouldn't* have."

"And if Bill Laverly had been the lucky purchaser, as he wanted to be, would you have had lunch with him?"

I was cornered, but I had to be honest. I struggled for words. There didn't seem to be any truly appropriate ones—just truthful ones.

"Yes—yes, of course. That was the whole idea."

He lifted his hat to me with the same smile shining out of his eyes.

"You're a good sport, Elizabeth," he said. "See you in Lacombe." He replaced his hat and was gone.

A hired auto was waiting for us in Lacombe. It had been arranged for Phil so that the trip would not be too tiring. Because the family still clung together, I shared the front seat with Wynn who was driving. I'm sure that he noticed my silence, but he said nothing about it. Instead, he gave me a short Alberta biology lesson about the local flora and fauna. I found it all very interesting; in fact, he was providing some of the very information for which I had unsuccessfully searched in the Calgary library.

"Could you—would you mind coming to the school and telling some of this to the students?" I blurted out without thinking. "It's exactly what I've wanted to teach them, but I know so little—and I couldn't find any books."

"I'd love to," he said, and I was certain that he meant it, "but I'm leaving tomorrow. It's back to work for me on Wednesday."

"I see."

I sat silently. He spoke, "You can go ahead and use the little that I've told you; and the next time that I see you, I'll give you an additional lesson—how's that?"

My heart skipped—then made up for the lost beat in double time. I would be seeing him again.

"You come home often?"

"No—sometimes not for months, or even years. It depends on where I'm posted."

"And where will you be posted?"

"I don't know that yet."

"You don't know? You go back to work in two days, and you don't even know where?"

"I'll know in time to get to the place they want to send me."

"Then there may not be another lesson," I said dully. *I may not ever see him again,* my heart mourned.

"True," his voice as serious as mine, "there may not."

We drove in silence for a while. Suddenly he turned to me in excitement.

"Will Blake!" he exclaimed. "He's a real woodsman. If anyone knows about our area, Will does. He would be glad to come and speak to your pupils. Want me to talk to him?"

Disappointment seeped all through me. Couldn't he see that it was more than knowledge that I was interested in? Still, I appreciated the fact that he had bothered to consider the needs of my pupils. I forced a smile.

"That's fine," I said. "You'll be very busy. I'll talk to him. Thank you."

THIRTY

The Christmas Program

My students and I settled back into classroom routines. The air was colder now, so each morning I shivered my way through starting my own fire; and then, just when the teacherage was beginning to get comfortable, I had to leave the warmth of it and hurry across to the school to get the fire going there. It certainly helped to know how to handle the dampers properly. Even so, on some days I seemed to get more smoke than flame.

The students, for the most part, were working hard and making steady progress. Even the older boys were beginning to study seriously. Andy was still talked about in loving terms. We missed our cheering section.

In mid-November we began work in earnest on our Christmas program. The students were so eager to make a good showing that they coaxed me daily for a chance to practice. I thought that part of their enthusiasm might be due to the fact that rehearsal kept them from studying spelling and geography, so I vetoed the idea of spending too much time away from the books and encouraged them to learn their lines at home.

As the time for the performance drew near, we were all caught up in the excitement. First there would be the program. All of the students were involved in presentations. After that portion was over, Santa would make an appearance, and hand out eagerly awaited candy bags. Mr. Laverly had a committee in charge of the bags—and of arranging for Santa, and I was glad that they were not my responsibilities. I was sure that I would have all I could do to get the program and the school in order. After the arrival and departure of the jolly red elf, we would all enjoy a lunch together. It sounded simple enough, but it actually took hours and hours to prepare.

Whispers began to circulate among the girls as to what each would be wearing. Many even spoke of *new* dresses that their mammas were going to be making out of "Jane's old one" or "Sally's full skirt" and, in some cases, even brand-new material, purchased just for that purpose. It was easy to catch their excitement. If ever they felt in need of and entitled to a new dress, now was the time.

The boys said nothing about what they would be wearing. Instead, they talked of the new bells for the team harness or the fact that their pa had said that they could do the driving. It seemed that Christmas was an important time for beginning drivers.

We all hoped for good weather, for snow on the ground to make things pretty, and temperature not too cold for the teams. The people could bundle up, but the poor horses had to stand in the cold while they waited for the proceedings of the evening to end.

The night finally arrived, crisp and cold but clear. The wind was not blowing, and I felt thankful for that fact as I trudged through the snow on my various errands between the teacherage and schoolhouse. Each step squeaked and crunched in the dry snow.

I built the fire early so that the room would be comfortably warm, and put on two big kettles of water to heat. The pump handle was so cold that even through my woolen mittens, my hands complained.

I carried the pails of water carefully, knowing that water splashed on my skirt or shoes would be ice by the time I had finished my chore and would make for a most uncomfortable evening.

My breath preceded me in little wisps of silvery smoke, curling around my head as I moved forward. Overhead the stars shone so brightly that I felt I had only to reach out my hand to feel the warmth of them. As I walked toward the schoolhouse, one glittering star was shaken from its celestial bed and streaked earthward, leaving a long silver streamer trailing behind it.

In the distance I heard the wail of a coyote. They were not very close tonight. I waited for the answer of the pack, but it did not come. Perhaps the rest were snuggled closely together in an underground den.

By the time I heard the jingling of harness bells and the squealing of sleigh runners, the schoolroom was comfortably warm and the final preparations were complete. I straightened my hair, smoothed out the skirt of my green velvet dress that I had decided to bring with me from Calgary for this very night, and prepared to meet the first arrivals.

The women and children bustled into the schoolroom to be unbundled from their many wraps, while the men remained outside for a moment to care for the horses. Blankets that had been used to tuck in children were now thrown over animals, and hay was placed within the teams' reach. There was not enough room in our small barn, so many of the horses were tied to fence posts around the schoolyard.

The Christmas program went very well, all things considered. There were a few minor calamities: Mindy Blake forgot her lines and fled the make-shift stage in tears; Tim Mattoch, with his poor eyesight, tripped his way onto the platform, but he bounced back up and led the people in the laughter; Maudie Clark became confused in the drill and misled Olga Peterson and Ruthie Clark—soon the whole group was in a snarl, so I had to stop the whole thing and have them start over. Their second attempt was nearly flawless. Sally Clark did a wonderful job reciting "The Night Before Christmas," and little Else sang "Away in a Manger" in such a sweet, clear voice that it brought tears to more than a few eyes. Our playlet went well, too, and we had a most responsive audience. I'm sure that with the evening's performance each of the students felt like a star, and there were no parents there who would have argued with them.

When the program had ended, each of the students found a seat. It was now time for Santa to make an appearance. We waited, every ear straining, and then we heard a distant jingling of my hand-held school bell and a "ho-ho-ho." A cheer went up from all of the children in the group—I think that even some of the adults joined them.

Santa entered—red suit, whiskers, and all—with his ho-ho-ho ringing out merrily. He said a few muffled words to the children, asking if they had been good, to which they replied in chorus, "Yes!" He then went right to work calling out names and passing out the candy bags. At the sound of each name, a child bounded forward, eyes shining and hands reaching out eagerly. As the last child returned to her seat, I gave Mr. Laverly a nod—he was to thank our unknown Santa. But to my surprise, Santa produced another bag, this one from within his jacket. He called loudly, "Miss Elizabeth Thatcher."

I stood dumbstruck.

My students cheered and clapped.

"Miss Elizabeth Thatcher," Santa called again.

"C'mon, Teacher. C'mon," the students coaxed.

I could feel my face flushing, but I finally got to my feet and began moving toward Santa.

"C'mon now, Miss Thatcher," Santa echoed the children in a hearty, disguised voice. "Step right up here on the platform. Don't be shy, now."

With the help of several hands I found myself on the platform. I reached timidly for the brown bag in Santa's hand, but he pulled it back with another ho-ho-ho.

"Not so fast now, Miss Thatcher. Have you been a good girl?"

The children howled, and I blushed.

"I—I've tried to be," I answered.

"Has she, children?" Santa asked my little group. A big cheer went up, along with some shrill whistles. Santa ho-ho'ed again.

"Well, then I guess you can have it. But first give Santa a little kiss." He tapped his whiskered cheek with a gloved hand.

I'm not sure if my face was red or white at that point.

"C'mon now," he said, "give Santa a little kiss." He continued to point at his cheek. Cheers and howls filled the room.

I looked at the whiskered cheek, shrugged my shoulders slightly, and standing on tiptoe, planted a kiss on dear old Santa amid shouts, cheers, whistles, and clapping.

My face still red, I left the platform clutching the small brown bag. By the time I had regained my composure and my post by the brewing pot of coffee, Santa's ho-ho-ho's were fading in the distance.

We proceeded to serve the lunch. I poured coffee and hot chocolate. When I finally ran out of customers, I decided to have a cup of hot chocolate myself. Lydia Delaney motioned me over to her family. It was good to see Phil with more color in his cheeks, and he had gained a few pounds since I had last seen him. They made room for me between the two Mrs. Delaneys. They were anxious to know about my Christmas plans, and I told them that I intended to spend the holiday recess with Jon's family in Calgary.

I wanted to ask them about Wynn—where he had been posted and if they expected him home, but I didn't trust my voice to be casual enough, so I held my tongue.

A small stirring drew our attention to the far side of the room and I noticed Phillip, Sr. watching it with interest. Henry Laverly seemed to be circulating among the young men, prompting a number of them to dig disgustedly into their pockets. Phil stood up and sauntered toward them, greeting and talking with neighbors as he worked his way across the room.

It wasn't until after nearly all of the crowd had bundled up and headed for home, sleighbells ringing and harnesses crackling, that word reached me. It seemed that some of the neighborhood young men had made bets as to who would be the first to get a kiss from the new, young schoolteacher; and bashful, reserved Henry Laverly, with his sneaky Santa routine, had just collected the bets.

THIRTY-ONE
Christmas Eve

I didn't realize just how much I was looking forward to Christmas break until I climbed aboard the train in Lacombe and was finally bound for Calgary. A lonesomeness for my family back East swept over me in an almost overwhelming wave, and for a moment I considered buying a ticket for Toronto and heading home. My sense of reason, and my love for my students, held me steady, so instead I began to plan the days that I would spend with Jon and his family.

The train ride was, as usual, long and slow; and by the time we arrived in Calgary the short winter's day was almost spent, and darkness was creeping upon us.

Jon met me at the station. He had brought the three older children with him, and they all took turns trying to dislodge my hat with their wild bear hugs. My enthusiasm may have been more controlled but nonetheless sincere.

The family was preparing for Christmas. Festive decorations greeted us at the front door, and delicious odors reached us as soon as we stepped inside. It was like coming home, and my homesickness began to leave me.

The first days I spent in shopping and being entertained by the children. Sarah had to bring me up-to-date on her reading skills, and William demonstrated his ability on the violin, while Kathleen, chattering constantly, followed me about.

There was to be a special Christmas Eve service in the church, and the children talked about it constantly, probably as much from the opportunity to "stay up late" as anything else. By the time the day arrived, I, too, had caught their excitement.

We traveled the short distance by sleigh, for the cold weather made unpredictable the starting of automobiles left out in the elements. Besides, Mary maintained, the sleigh was much more in keeping with Christmas. The rest of us agreed. We burrowed together under furry buffalo robes and enjoyed the twinkling of the stars in the clear sky overhead and the crisp sound of the snow under the runners.

The team, a pair of magnificent bays, snorted and tossed their heads, sending out small clouds of frosty breath. I had the feeling that the two would have enjoyed a good run, so I was glad that Jon was well able to handle them.

Jon seated us quite near the front of the church. I sat nestled between Sarah on my left and Kathleen on my right. The room was glowing with candlelight; shadows danced across the faces of the two playing the parts of Mary and Joseph and looking down on the Christ Child lying in the manger bed. The green wreaths made of spruce not only looked Christmasy, but they brought a lovely Christmasy smell to the sanctuary as well.

The service was delightful. We sensed again the awe of the first Christmas so long ago when God sent His most precious gift, His Son Jesus, into the world to be born of a woman so that someday, as a sacrifice, He could provide salvation for the whole human race.

The familiar Christmas carols had never meant as much to me as they did on that night. As I recited the words, I pictured the young Mary, her hour having come, with no one to care for her—no warm bed, no private room, no skilled midwife—only straw, a stable, and an anxious husband nearby. She herself cared for the newborn Son of God, the baby Jesus.

I thought of my Lord, the Maker of Heaven and Earth, now reduced to a helpless child, not even able to express His needs and wants, far less demand the honor due Him; and I thought of the Father who must have watched anxiously from His throne as the new Babe made His appearance in the world that He had fashioned. God himself lay snuggled against the breast of a young peasant girl in a dimly lit stable in Bethlehem. How God must have loved mankind, to allow Him to come.

I left the service that night with a full heart and overflowing eyes. I brushed away tears with my handkerchief as I smiled at Kathleen and Sarah.

"Baby 'Liz'beth wasn't born with the cows," Kathleen whispered.

I nodded my head and gave her a squeeze to let her know that I knew how she felt.

"I'm glad," she insisted. She thought silently for a few minutes, then continued, "If she would have been, would she have been a Jesus?"

I smiled. "No, dear, she still would have been an Elizabeth. And Jesus would have still been Jesus, the Son of God, if He had been born in a hospital room or a King's chamber. Where one is born doesn't change who one is. But God knew where Jesus would be born, so He told us through His prophet, many years before it actually happened."

"God's pretty smart, huh?"

"Yes, Kathleen. God knows *all* things."

We followed the others down the aisle. The candle flames flickered and wavered, sending light and shadow to play on smiling faces while friends greeted one another as they moved toward the door.

"Hello, Elizabeth."

At the sound of the familiar voice, I turned quickly around and found myself looking up into the face of Wynn. It was the first time I had seen him in uniform. If I had found it difficult before to imagine him as a Mountie, as I looked at him now I could not imagine him as anything else. His strength was more than physical. There was a strength of character and purpose about him that made the red tunic look deserving of the man.

My breath had caught in a little gasp and it was a moment before I could answer him.

"I wasn't expecting to see you," I said shyly, and his widening smile brought a flush to my cheeks.

By then Kathleen had realized who was beside us and had claimed his attention. Jerking his sleeve, she was demanding, "Are you coming to our house, Dee? Are you coming to see our tree?"

"Hey," he said, "slow down, Moppet. As a matter of fact, your mother has invited me to your house, and I think—" he teased lightly, "I think *maybe* I'll come."

She ignored his teasing and clapped her hands. "He's coming, Aunt Beth! Isn't that good?"

I was busy trying to understand the strange fluttering of my heart. Was it the aura of the red jacket, or the fact that he had spoken my name? I hoped that Kathleen could keep his attention until I was able to get myself well under control.

Mary called Kathleen and the girl went to join her family. I was left, heart thumping, standing very close in the crowded aisle to this awesome man in the red coat.

"Jon has suggested," he began, and then his eyes began to twinkle, "—no, that's not true. Jon has agreed to *my* suggestion that, since I am to spend the evening at his house, you could ride over with me so that I might catch up on the Pine Springs news." He laughed then—a soft, good-natured chuckle. "Maybe that's not entirely true either, but I do want a chance for a bit of a talk, because once we get to Jon's and in the company of his chattering offspring, there will be little chance to even ask how you've been."

I smiled, knowing that he was right.

"Would you, Elizabeth?"

My smile seemed to wobble a little. "I'd like that."

He took my arm and steered me through the crowd and out to his waiting team. As the team stomped impatiently, the bells on their harness jingled clearly through the night air and seemed to echo again and again from the nearby buildings.

Wynn helped me into the sleigh and tucked the robes closely about me. As soon as we were on our way, he opened the conversation.

"So how is my big brother?"

"He's fine. I saw him and the family just a few nights ago at the Christmas program. He looks much better—has gained weight and picked up some color—and he looks absolutely happy."

"Good," was all he answered, but he spoke the single word with great feeling.

We were silent for several moments. I held my tongue, and my breath, until I feared that I would burst. I gave up. I had to know.

"And are you posted here in Calgary?"

"For now, but I'm not sure for how long. I expect that another posting will come soon, though I don't know where. I'm enjoying Calgary. The city is growing so fast that there's always something going on, but I'm rather anxious to get back—"

"Back to where?"

"I've spent six years at various posts in the North. I like it there."

"What do you do? I didn't think that there were many settlers in the North."

"Settlers, no—not too many. Trappers mostly. But the North is full of people. We are far more than law enforcement to the people there; Mounties are the only dentists, doctors, coroners, arbitrators, advisors—and clergymen, that many of the people have. They depend upon us, Elizabeth, not just to bring justice but to bring hope and help."

I thought about his words, and I thought about Julie. I wondered if her impression of the scarlet-coated Mountie was so accurate after all. Rather than adventure and excitement, their job sounded like a great deal of responsibility and hard work to me. And it sounded noble, though I didn't think that Wynn Delaney would care for that word, so I kept it to myself.

"Are there many women there?" The words were out before I could stop them.

"White women? No. Very few. Oh, a few of the North West Mounted Police have taken brides—unwisely."

"Unwisely?"

"It's a very difficult life. No modern homes, no shops, no

entertainment. Often there are no white friends, unless it's a trapper's wife. It's not the place for a lady."

"But don't they need schools?"

"There are some mission schools, often taught by men. But for the most part, no—they don't think much about needing schools. The men know how to hunt and fish and care for their traps, and the women know how to tan the hides, dry the meat, haul the wood, tote the water. What more do they need to know? Those are the things necessary for surviving in their land."

I could tell by his voice that he was smiling as he said the words, yet I knew he was speaking from firsthand knowledge; he had worked among the people of the North. I did not try to argue.

He suddenly turned to me. "Here we are almost to Jon's, and you were to have given me all the news from Pine Springs. You'd better fill me in quickly," he prompted.

I laughed, and in as few words as possible I told him of some of the happenings of the community.

We pulled up to the front door and he stopped the team and helped me out of the sleigh. I had taken his offered arm to ease myself to the snow-packed ground when my foot caught in the buffalo robe. I tumbled forward, grabbing frantically for something solid. His reactions were quicker than mine, and before I could right myself I was held firmly in two strong arms.

"Are you all right?" he asked anxiously against my hair. I quickly steadied myself and gently pushed myself away from him.

"Just clumsy," I said in embarrassment. I released my hold on his coat sleeves and stepped back. I was thankful that he could not clearly see my face.

"It's slippery under foot," he cautioned.

"I'll *try* to be careful." I even managed a slight laugh.

"As soon as I care for the team, I'll be in."

I went quietly up the stairs to my room. In front of a mirror I removed my hat that had been jarred askew by my fall against Wynn. Straightening my hair with a trembling hand, I gave myself a few moments to regain my composure. By the time I arrived downstairs to join the family, Wynn was already there. Our eyes met briefly but neither of us made any comment.

Mary was serving cocoa and popcorn, and the children were jostling for a position close to the fire. As soon as they had finished their refreshments, Mary led them off to bed.

We spent the rest of the evening chatting and playing dominoes. It was nearly ten o'clock when Mary brought the coffee and Christmas baking. Jon threw more wood on the fire, and we pulled up close to the crackling flames and comfortably visited. At length, Mary asked Wynn, "Are you going to the wedding?"

He nodded.

"You don't seem very enthusiastic," she teased.

He still said nothing.

"So, why not?" Mary persisted.

"It's none of my business, I suppose," Wynn said slowly, "but I think that it's a mistake."

"Whose mistake?" Jon asked.

"Withers'."

"Is Withers the young Mountie?"

Wynn nodded.

"Mistake—how?" Mary asked, puzzled.

"You are a pest," Wynn teased. He stood up and moved closer to the fire. "Okay—I've said it before; here it is for you again. Withers is posted at Peace River—his young bride comes from Montreal. She is used to plays and concerts and dinner parties. She's trading that for blizzards and sickness, wild animals and loneliness. Do you think that she'll be able to appreciate the exchange? Come on, Mary—even *love* can't stand a test like that."

"Some women have done it, you know. Wynn, you might be short-selling love."

He turned back to the fire. "Yes," he said slowly, "some have. But I'd never want to ask it of the woman I loved."

I could tell that he truly meant those words, and something deep down inside of me began to weep. But Mary didn't let Wynn have the last word.

"Then you would also be short-selling the woman you loved," she said softly, *"if* she really loved you."

Wynn shook his head slightly, but his eyes did not turn from the fire.

THIRTY-TWO

Christmas Day

Christmas Day dawned bright and glistening. During the night there had been a fresh fall of snow, and the cleaned-up-world shimmered in the rays of the winter sun.

The day began early with the glad shrieks of the children as they discovered the gifts that were in their stockings and under the tree. We enjoyed a leisurely morning of games, nut roasting, and chatter. Dinner was to be served at one o'clock. Wynn joined us for dinner and he presented each of the children with a package. Jon, Mary, and I were each given fur mittens made by Wynn's northern Indian friends; I looked forward to using mine.

In the afternoon the children begged for a chance to try their new Christmas sleds. So, following Mary's suggestion, Wynn and I accompanied Jon when he took them to the hill. We all bundled up—I was glad for this opportunity to wear my new mittens—until we could barely waddle and headed out, laughing and jostling, for the hillside.

At the hill we all rode on the sleds. I was soon exhausted after the breathless rides and long return climbs. I decided to sit down on a fallen log partway up the hill and rest while the others enjoyed another ride.

I could hear the shrieks and laughter as they sped downward, Jon and Sarah on one sleigh, Wynn and Kathleen on another, and William on his own.

A few birds fluttered in a nearby tree and two squirrels fought over winter provisions. I leaned back against a tree and enjoyed the sparkling freshness of the winter air.

I could hear the children's chatter at the foot of the hill when Wynn suddenly swung into sight.

"Jon said that I should take you up to the top of the ridge and give you a look at the mountains."

"Oh," I cried, springing up eagerly, "can you see them from here?"

"From right up there," he answered, pointing above and beyond us.

"Then lead the way—I'd love to see them."

The loose snow made climbing difficult. Wynn stopped often to let me catch my breath, and a couple of times he held out his hand to me to help me over a fallen tree or up a particularly steep place.

At the top I discovered that the climb had been worth every step. Stretched out before us, their snow-capped peaks glistening in the winter sun, were the magnificent Rockies. I caught my breath in awe.

"Someday," I said softly, "I'm going to visit those mountains—and have a picnic lunch right up there at the timberline."

Wynn laughed.

"That's quite a hike up to the timberline, Elizabeth," he cautioned.

"Well, I don't care. It'll be worth it."

"How about settling for a picnic lunch beside a mountain stream instead—or at the base of Bow Falls or maybe among the rocks of Johnson Canyon?"

"You've been there—to all of those places?"

"Several times."

"Is it as beautiful as I imagine?"

"Unless you have a very exceptional imagination, it's even more beautiful."

"Oh, I'd love to see it!"

"Then you must. I wish that I could promise to take you but . . ."

Reluctantly I turned from the scene of the mountains to make my way back down the slope to Jon and the children. My thoughts were more on Wynn's unfinished sentence than on where I was placing my feet. He was so determined, so definite. He left no room at all for feelings, for caring. Somehow I felt that there should be something I could say or do to make him at least rethink his position, but I couldn't think of what it might be—at least not while I was scrambling down a steep hillside behind a man used to walking in such terrain.

Suddenly my foot slipped on a snow-covered log and my ankle twisted beneath me. I sat down to catch my breath and test the extent of the injury. To my relief, nothing much seemed wrong. I knew that nothing was broken, and I was sure that there was not even a serious sprain—just a bit of a twist. I was rising to my feet to hurry after Wynn when he looked back to check on my progress.

"What's the matter?" he called, his voice concerned.

I tried to respond lightly, "I'm fine—just twisted my ankle a bit."

I took a step but he stopped me.

"Stay where you are, Elizabeth, until I check out that ankle."

"But it's fine—"

"Let's be sure."

He was hurrying back up the hill toward me when a strange idea entered my head. Maybe this was a way to delay him for a few moments until I had fully considered what I could say. I sat back down on the tree stump and stared at my foot.

Wynn had been only a few steps ahead of me, breaking trail, so he was soon down on a knee before me. "Which one?" he asked, and I pointed to the left ankle.

He lifted it with gentle firmness and removed my boot. Carefully he began to feel the injured ankle, his fingers sensitive and gentle.

"Nothing broken." He squeezed. "Does this hurt?"

It did—slightly, though not enough to make me wince as hard as I did. I said nothing—just nodded my head in the affirmative. After all, he hadn't asked how *much* it hurt.

Wynn surveyed the trail ahead.

"It's only a few more steps until we are on the level. Can you make it?"

I knew that I could, but I didn't say so. Instead, I murmured, "If you could help me just a bit . . ."

He replaced my boot, leaving the laces loose.

"Too much pressure?" he asked.

"No—no—that's fine."

"Good. We wouldn't want to take a chance on frostbite as well. Are you ready?"

I had visions of limping down the trail with Wynn's arm supporting me. *Surely,* I thought, *under such conditions it should be easy to think of the right thing to say to this man.* But instead of offering his assistance, Wynn swept me up into his arms in one quick, gentle movement. The suddenness of it startled me, and I threw my arms around his neck.

"It's all right," he reassured me. "It's only a few steps down this bit of a bank, and we'll be on the level."

"But I—"

"I could throw you over my shoulder and carry you dead-man style," he teased.

"I think I would prefer—" I was going to say, "to walk," but that wasn't true, so I lamely stopped.

"So would I, Elizabeth," he said with his slow smile and looked deeply into my eyes.

That was when I should have made my little speech, but my brain was hazy and my lips dumb. I could think only of this moment—nothing more—and I rested my cheek against his coat and allowed myself this bliss that would in the future be a beautiful memory.

All too soon we were at the slope where Jon and the children were still sledding. Wynn put me down, cautious that I would not put my weight on my left foot. For one confused moment I could not remember which foot was supposed to be injured and had to look at my boot to see which one had the untied laces.

We had not spoken to one another for several minutes. As he lowered me to a seat on a log, his cheek brushed lightly against mine, and I feared that he would surely hear the throbbing of my heart.

"How is it?" he asked. "I hope I didn't jar it."

"Oh, no. You were most careful. I don't see how you were able to come down there so—" I couldn't finish.

"We'll get you home as quickly as possible," he promised, and he waved to William who came trudging up the slope with his sled.

Wynn insisted that I ride home on the sleigh, and I could hardly refuse. To insist upon walking would have given my ruse away, so I rode the sled, feeling foolish and deceptive.

When we arrived at the house, Wynn carried me in and deposited me on the couch. He suggested that ice packs might make my ankle more comfortable. Soon to be on duty, he couldn't stay for the evening. After promising to stop by to check on me at his first opportunity, he left.

I feigned a limp whenever I moved around for the rest of the day. It was hard to keep Jon and Mary from calling a doctor. I would have been mortified if one had been summoned on Christmas Day to look at my "injury." When bedtime finally arrived, I was relieved to take my perfectly fine ankle, and my guilty conscience, to the privacy of my own room.

I went to bed troubled. I could feel again the roughness of Wynn's wool coat against my cheek, and the strength of his arms supporting me as he carried me. I realized that I unwillingly had fallen in love with the man; and I might have missed my only opportunity to plead my case. Still, if a man was determined not to care for a woman, what could she possibly say to change his mind? I had no idea, having never been in such a position till now. For a moment I wished that I had learned a few of the feminine ploys that Julie used to such advantage, then checked myself. I had already used more trickery than I could feel comfortable with. What in the world had ever possessed me to make me promote such a falsehood? Shame flushed my cheeks. Never would I resort to such devious tactics again.

THIRTY-THREE

The Confession

The next morning I lightly brushed aside the inquiries concerning my ankle and assured everyone that it was just fine. I was embarrassed over the whole affair and was not anxious to discuss it. Mary insisted that I stay off my feet; so to appease her and to escape from everyone's sympathy, I retreated to Jon's library where I buried myself in a good book.

About noon, Jon entered with William reluctantly in tow. One look at their faces, and I could see that it was to be a serious discussion. I rose to excuse myself but Jon stopped me.

"Sit still, Beth. We'll only be a few moments. No need for you to bother that ankle of yours."

There it was again—my poor ankle. I flushed and was glad that the book hid my face. My guilt must certainly have shown.

Jon sat down and pulled William to him.

"Now, Son, what explanation do you have? Do you realize that what you've done is wrong?"

"Yes."

"Do you realize that what you've done is *sin*?"

"It's not *that* wrong."

"Oh, yes, it is. God has said, 'Thou shalt not,' but you did. Now, doesn't that make it sin?"

"Well, it wasn't a very *big* sin," William argued.

"There are no 'big' or 'little' sins, Son. God hasn't divided them up that way. Sin is—sin. Do you know how God feels about sin?"

William nodded his head in the affirmative, but the stubborn look lingered in his eyes.

"He don't like it."

"Right—He doesn't like it. Do you know *why* He hates it so much?"

" 'Cause He's God?" William asked.

"Yes, He's God, and He's righteous and pure and good. There is nothing false or wrong or hurtful in the character of God. But I think there is an even *bigger* reason why God hates sin so much."

William's eyes were wide as they studied his father's face.

"It's because sin cost Him the life of His Son, Jesus. God decreed that those who sin must die. Man sinned—but God still loved him. God didn't want man to die for his sin, so God provided a substitute. If man accepted the fact that another had died in his place, and was truly sorry for his sin, then he wouldn't have to die."

"I know that," William said, his lip trembling. Jon's arm went around his son's waist.

"Many times," Jon continued, "folks get the idea that it was only the big sins, like murder and idol worship, that made it necessary for Jesus to die. But it wasn't, Son. It was, and is, any and *all* sin. If there had been any other way, if our holy God could have ignored sin, or blinked at it, or turned His head, or pretended that it just hadn't happened or didn't matter, then He would never, never have sent Jesus to die. God loved His Son—yet the death of His Son was the only way for God to spare us from the penalty of death that we deserve. He *loves* us. So that's why God hates sin—all sin, because it meant death for His Son. And if we still hang on to our sin, it means that we don't value what Jesus did for us."

"But I do," William protested. "I didn't mean to hurt Jesus—honest." A tear coursed down each cheek. Jon pulled the boy close.

"I know you didn't, Son. We often hurt God without meaning to. Now I want you to tell God that you didn't mean it, and that you are sorry, and that with His help you will not do it again. After that, we will go and have a talk with Stacy."

"Do I have to?" William pleaded. "Do I have to go to Stacy? I'll talk to God, Pa—but can't *you* tell Stacy?"

"No, Son. Part of being forgiven is making things right. God asks that of us—always. It's called 'restitution.' If Jesus was willing to pay the death penalty for us, to make things right between us and God, then it's not too much for God to ask that we make things right between ourselves and whomever we have wronged."

They knelt together by Jon's big chair, and a tearful William asked God's forgiveness. Then hand-in-hand, they left the room to go speak with Stacy, the kitchen helper.

I never did discover what William's wrong was. It did not seem important—for pricking at my own conscience was my dishonesty of the day before. I looked down at my ankle, feeling a hatred for the offending member; then I reminded myself that it wasn't the ankle that was at fault.

I was called for lunch. William appeared at the table, all traces of tears gone. In fact, he looked happier than usual, and when Stacy served the dessert, I noticed that William received a larger-than-usual serving. William noticed it, and he gave Stacy a grin. She winked—ever so quickly and slyly. Repentance, confession, and restitution. William knew all about the benefits, while I still sat miserable and squirming in my chair.

After lunch I went to my room. It seemed that my battle lasted most of the afternoon. I was like William. I didn't mind telling my wrongdoing to God, but to speak to Wynn? The very thought of it made my cheeks burn. Yet, plead as I would for God's forgiveness, I had no peace of heart. Confession—confession—kept ringing in my mind. Finally I threw myself upon my bed in desperation.

"God, it was such a foolish little thing," I pleaded.

"It was a *wrong* thing," my conscience answered.

"Yes, it was wrong—"

"It was sin. You *chose* to make someone believe an untruth."

"But the untruth will hurt no one."

"How can you speak of *hurt*? It cost Jesus His life."

"But—please don't make me talk to Wynn—not Wynn. Do you know what he'll think of me?"

"Do you care what God thinks of you?"

"Of course, but . . ."

I wept, I pleaded, I argued, but at length I gave in.

"Okay, if that's what must be, I will confess to Wynn at my first opportunity."

Peace came, but my dread of the encounter with Wynn did not go away.

I did not need to be in misery for long, for Wynn dropped by that evening to check on my "injured" ankle. He was only passing by, he said, so couldn't stay. After exchanging a few words with Jon and Mary, he picked up his fur winter hat and prepared to leave. I swallowed hard and stood up. My face felt hot and my throat dry.

"I must see you for a moment—please."

There was just a flicker of surprise—or concern—on his face.

"Of course."

I led the way to Jon's library, making sure that I, in no way, favored my "injured" ankle. Once inside, I closed the door and faced him. I wanted to run away, to hide my face, to lie again—anything but to face this man with the truth. Before I could change my mind and do any one of those things, I plunged in.

"I have a confession—about my ankle. I didn't injure it. I pretended. It's fine—I—" I dropped my gaze. No longer could I look into those honest, blue eyes. I turned slightly from him.

"I didn't think you would carry me. I just wanted—a little—a little more time . . ." I knew that I had to be honest, as much as it humbled me. "I acted like a silly child," I said, making myself look straight into his eyes. "I guess—I guess—I—I wanted your attention—and I—I didn't know how else to get it. I know it was foolish—and I'm—I'm sorry."

Wynn was looking directly at me. His eyes did not scorn or mock me, nor did he look shocked or disgusted. There was an understanding—and, yes, a softness that I had not expected to see. I turned from him lest I would do something very foolish—such as cry, or throw myself into his arms.

"I have confessed my dishonesty to God—and asked for His forgiveness. He has graciously granted it. Now—" My voice was almost a whisper, "now I would like to ask *your* forgiveness, also."

I felt Wynn's hands on my shoulders and he turned me gently to face him.

"Elizabeth," he said softly, "I can't tell you how much I respect you for what you've just done. Few people—" he hesitated a moment. "You've asked for my forgiveness. I give it—willingly, and now I, in turn, must ask yours."

I know that surprise must have shown on my face.

"Elizabeth, I examined your ankle—remember?"

I nodded.

"It was my choice to carry you—right?"

I just looked at him, not able to follow his thinking.

"Elizabeth, I am trained in first aid—to recognize breaks, and injuries, and sprains—"

I understood then.

"You *knew* . . . ?"

He nodded, his eyes not leaving mine. I turned from him, confused. What was he saying? He knew that my ankle was not injured when he examined it, yet he had carried me and held me close against his chest. Was it to shame me? To see how far I would let the charade go?

"Why?"

As I spoke, my back was still toward him. He paced to the window where he stood looking out on the darkness.

"Why?" he echoed. "I should think it rather obvious."

He stood for a moment, and then, his somber mood changed. He crossed back to me, his Mounties' hat in his hand ready to be placed on his head. I knew that he was leaving. The twinkle of humor had returned to his eyes and made the corner of his lips twitch slightly.

"And frankly, Elizabeth," he said through that controlled smile, "I've never enjoyed anything more." And with a slight nod he departed, and the door closed softly behind him.

THIRTY-FOUR

Return to Pine Springs

I saw Wynn a number of times that week. Neither of us ever mentioned my ankle. Nor were we ever alone. All of our time together was shared with Jon or Mary or one of the children.

But I learned much about him; that he loved people, young and old alike; that he was respected—by White and Indian; that he was knowledgeable, seeming to know something about almost everything; that he read widely and was able to converse about science as easily as he could recite poetry; that he had a deep and solid faith in God; and that he sensed a mission to help those whom many believed to be second-rate citizens. The more I knew of him the more I admired him, and what had previously been an infatuation was daily turning into a feeling much more deep and permanent.

He was kind to me, even solicitous. He even seemed to enjoy my company, but never once did he give me reason to believe that he had changed his mind concerning his conviction that marriage was unwise for a Mountie.

I couldn't understand how a man could be so stubborn, and if I hadn't already learned to love him so much, I would angrily and painfully have dismissed him from my thoughts.

Reluctantly I packed my bags and prepared for my trip back to Pine Springs. Mr. Laverly had promised to have someone meet my train at Lacombe.

I spent the entire long journey trying to make some sense out of my feelings for Wynn. It was not the least bit difficult for me to understand why a woman would fall for such a man—but why she should persist against such an obvious stone wall of stubborn determination to remain single was beyond me. Perhaps, I reasoned, I preferred his polite, enjoyable company to the alternative of not being with him at all.

Bill Laverly stood on the platform, his smile stretched from ear to ear, when I descended from the train. He was the last person I wanted to see, but what could I do? He loaded my suitcases and tucked me in with a bearskin rug, taking far too much time in the process, I thought.

He had talked his father into buying a light cutter and I knew, before we even moved out of the town, that I was in for the ride of my life. Bill cracked a whip over the team, and we jerked away in a swirl of snow, bells jingling and horses snorting. My only consolation was that the faster we went, the sooner I would be home and away from the company of this grinning, speed-mad man.

He seemed to be continually looking at me and adjusting the bearskins, but when he dared to put his arm across the back of the seat behind me, I drew the line. Drawing myself away from him, I informed him that I would be much more comfortable if he used *both* hands to guide the racing team.

As we entered the lane to the teacherage, I noticed smoke coming from the chimney. *Surely Bill hadn't lit the fire before he left,* was my first thought. Bill might like a pretty face, but thoughtful he was not.

After he had pulled the team to a snow-swirling stop, he drew out my suitcases, handed them to me and then with a scraping swish, he spun the cutter around and headed his galloping team for home. "See ya!" he yelled over his shoulder, his wide grin still spread across his face.

When I entered the little house it was easy to tell who had been there. The fire was burning cheerily, foodstuffs were arranged neatly on the cupboard, and my table was adorned with fresh coffeecake—Anna's specialty. A small pot of stew simmered near the back of the stove and the teakettle hummed merrily. How nice to be welcomed home, and how cold and miserable it would have been to enter the house that had seen no occupant or fire for two weeks.

While I ate the hot stew and fresh bread, my mind did a complete shift. I was anxious to get back to my students and the classroom. Faces flashed before me, and I thought of the achievements and the needs of each one. I was proud of my students. They had already accomplished so much in the short time that we had been together. I promised that I would do my very best for them in the months that lay ahead.

THIRTY-FIVE

Spring

The pupils seemed to share my enthusiasm. The next few months went very quickly, with our total concentration being given to our teaching and learning.

In March we had a visit from the district inspector. I don't know who was more nervous—my students or I.

Mr. Matthews, a tall, thin man with a pinched face, quick, dark eyes, and a high-pitched voice, spoke loudly, as though that would give him added authority. All the while that I taught that day, I could feel those sharp eyes on me, boring, probing, and even daring me. By lunch hour I was already exhausted, but he pulled a bench up close to my desk and began questioning me.

In the afternoon he shifted his attention to my pupils, quizzing them and calling on them to work sums or read a passage. I watched the poor, frightened children squirm and sweat, and I wished, for their sakes as well as my own, that the man would go away. Eventually he did, and all of us sighed and then laughed together in an effort to shake off our tension. I dismissed the class early for home.

The next day I had another visitor. Wynn had come to see Phil and Lydia, so he stopped by the school to deliver a note from Mary. I wished that I could invite him to the teacherage for supper, or at least tea, but I knew that such was forbidden and perhaps unwise, as well. We chatted of general things, and he waited while I wrote a quick note for him to take back to Mary. He had not yet received another posting. Just as my heart sang at the news, he stilled the song by informing me that it was bound to come, though he knew not when. One of the other fellows had just left for Lac La Biche, he said, and another Mountie who had been in Calgary for three years had just received a posting to Grouard, on Lesser Slave Lake.

"Did they have families?" I asked—not "wives," but "families"—hoping that Wynn would not guess my thoughts.

"McKenzie did—a wife and a young son."

"Did they mind going?"

"She didn't seem to, but she's been north before."

One point for me, I thought. He had had to admit that there was at least one woman who didn't mind going north with her husband. But Wynn went on.

"Aitcheson had a girl. When his posting came in, she called off the wedding."

My heart sank.

I wanted to say, "Well, some women can handle it—others can't." But I said nothing.

When Wynn left, he surprised me by giving me a compliment, at least it seemed like one to me.

"I think that this country life must agree with you, Elizabeth. You look more healthy and pretty every time I see you."

Healthy and pretty! It wasn't exactly as if he had declared me beautiful, but it was close—and coming from Wynn, who wasn't given to flattery, I decided to regard it as special.

I hummed happily after he had left.

Easter's arrival nearly caught me unawares, in the midst of my busyness. I packed for a trip to Jon and Mary's, anticipating a wonderful time in the city. I did enjoy the change and being with my family, but the fact that Wynn was spending time at Regina took much of the pleasure out of my holiday.

Mary delighted in letting slip frequent references to Wynn and his obvious high regard for me. I couldn't see how Mary could come to such conclusions, and I did wish that she would stop her nonsense. She seemed to be of the opinion that if I'd just show Wynn that I truly cared for him, he would shelve all his previous opinions regarding marriage and declare his undying love. I wasn't about to throw myself at any man, Wynn Delaney included; and besides, I was convinced that to do so would accomplish nothing, other than making a complete fool of myself.

I spent the week shopping, reading, loafing, playing with the children, and snuggling Baby Elizabeth. At the end of the week I was eager to return to the classroom. I had not asked Mr. Laverly for a ride from the Lacombe station, nor even informed him of the train on which I would arrive. My plan was to hire Pearlie's father to drive me out in his automobile. When I alighted from the train I discovered that the Clarks were in town. They kindly offered me a ride, which I gladly accepted.

Upon arriving at my teacherage, I built my own fire, fixed a simple supper, and then went to the schoolhouse. I wanted to get an early start on lesson preparations for the last few weeks of the school term.

Wynn mailed me a book—or rather, a manual, which I imagined was used by the North West Mounted Police. It contained many facts about Alberta, including its vegetation, animals and their behavior, the peoples and their way of life, and industry. I found it fascinating—especially since it had come from Wynn. His short note had stated that he thought I might find the information interesting and helpful. I did. I used much of the book in my classes. The students and I took advantage of the early spring weather to go on a nature hike and identify the growth according to the manual.

April passed into May, and May into June. The wild roses began to appear, first as scattered blooms and then as walls of blossoms beside the roadway. The children hunted strawberries, which they shared with me, delivering them in sticky, dirty palms. It was a delightful time of year, and I gloried in each sun-splashed new day, hearing, seeing, and breathing the newborn summer.

The families of the school children began another round of have-the-teacher-in-for-supper. I loved this time. I loved the people. I loved my visits in their homes. I loved the walks in the pleasant sunshine, to and from their farms. I loved the family chatter around the table. It was much nicer than living and eating alone.

It was a Friday evening and I had been invited to the Blakes. We enjoyed a pleasant meal together. Mrs. Blake had fixed roast chicken, and the girls had found enough strawberries to supply a somewhat skimpy shortcake. I lingered awhile over a cup of coffee and then reluctantly started for home.

After walking down the road for about a quarter of a mile, I came to the shortcut through the trees which the Blake children used to reach the school. I decided that nothing would be more delightful than a stroll through the woods on a warm, pleasant evening, so I left the road and started down the path. I had not gone far when I heard a commotion on the trail ahead of me. I cautiously took a few more steps; right before my eyes was a *bear,* busily rolling over a dead log. I knew that it was a bear—there was no doubting that—though what he was doing in these woods I could not for the life of me imagine. No bears that I had heard of had ever been seen here. I tried to remember what Wynn's book had said about bears, and I tried to determine what kind of a bear this one was, but my mind would not work.

The bear spied me at about the same instant that I spied him. We were only a short distance from one another. I wasn't sure who had startled whom the most. The bear suddenly gave a grunt and rose up on his hind legs. He looked mammoth. I wanted to run but my legs had turned to jelly. I wanted to scream but my mouth would not open, and my throat closed up on the sound.

The bear stood there, swinging his big head back and forth, sniffing and growling, his front paws held in readiness before him. Then he took a step toward me, snorting as he did so—and I felt my world going black. I crumpled to the earth in total darkness.

When I began to revive I sensed that I was moving, being carried in strong arms. For one terrifying minute I thought that it might be the bear toting me off. I fought to regain consciousness. My eyes slowly focused. It was Wynn.

"Steady, Elizabeth. It's all right." His arm tightened about me. I turned my face against him and began to cry.

He carried me out to the roadway and then lowered me to my feet, but he did not let me go. He pulled me close and let me shiver and weep until I began to regain some sense. All this time he had held me and stroked my hair or patted my shoulder, saying, "It's all right now, Elizabeth—you're fine—you're with me—it's gone—it's gone."

Finally I had control of myself enough to stand on my own feet and speak.

"A bear—"

"I know," he said, "I saw him."

"I was going to take the shortcut," I babbled on.

"I saw you."

"Where'd you come from?"

"I was driving to your house when I saw you leave the road. I left the automobile and ran after you, so that I could give you a ride home. Just as I caught up with you I saw—"

"The bear."

"Yes, the bear. I was going to call out to you, but I was afraid that you might run—running is the worst thing that one can do."

"I couldn't run—I couldn't . . ." and I started to sob again. The world was whirling and my knees were getting weak. I clung to Wynn, my thoughts back with that reared-up bear slowly advancing toward me.

Wynn's arms tightened about me and then I was being kissed—a kiss that drove all thought of the bear far from my mind. Slowly my arm stole up and around the back of Wynn's neck. I floated in a world where only Wynn and I existed, a world that I never wanted to end. But it did. Wynn stopped kissing me and swung me into his arms and carried me to the auto that was waiting on the roadway.

"Your mother sent a parcel to Jon and Mary," he said matter-of-factly as he walked. "She included a number of things for you, so, as I had a couple of days off, Jon suggested that I borrow his vehicle, visit my brother, and deliver the packages to you."

"I see," I murmured against Wynn's shirt front as he lifted me to the seat of the car, then went around to climb in beside me—but I didn't see. I was still far too busy remembering Wynn's kiss. I expected him to start the automobile, but he didn't. Instead, he hesitated, and I dared to hope that he might kiss me again. Instead, he cleared his throat to speak, reaching for my hand and holding it.

"Elizabeth, I owe you an apology."

Startled, I came back to full consciousness.

"I had no right to kiss you like that—I know that. And I didn't mean by it—" He stopped and gazed at me. "I could see that you were thinking again of that bear—your face was going white and your eyes looked terrified, and I thought that you might faint again. I had to make you think of something else, to get your mind off the bear; and the only thing that I could think to do—well—I—I kissed you."

Slowly the words sank in. At first they had made no sense, but the sting of them began to reach through my numbed senses. Wynn had kissed me just for the medical benefit of snapping me out of shock. But that wasn't how I had kissed him. Surely he had been aware of my response, my eagerness. Oh, yes, he would have been aware all right, and now he was apologizing for having kissed me at all! He wanted to be sure that I knew that he meant nothing personal by the kiss and to point out that the response on my part had been ridiculous and unfounded. He was still Mr. Mountie, married to his profession, and a mere, hapless schoolteacher was not about to turn his head.

With one quick motion I jerked back my hand.

"No man ever *has* to kiss me—not for *any* reason," I threw at him. "I would rather have been mauled by that bear than to be so—so indebted to you, Mr. Delaney!" I jumped from the auto and ran blindly across the ditch and down the pathway from which I had just been rescued.

I did remember the bear, but in my anger I was convinced that he would be no match for me. I heard Wynn call my name, but the sound only made me more angry and my tears fall more freely. The nerve of the man to get me to throw my love at his feet and then turn his back upon me with a trite apology! I would never, never, never look at him again.

Phillip, Jr. brought the gifts from my mother to school the next day. The package only helped to heighten my new resolve to return home. The East was where I belonged.

THIRTY-SIX

School Ends

My determination to put Wynn from my mind did not make it any easier to accomplish the fact. I thought of him constantly. I loved him, hated him, forgave him, scorned him, and pined for him by turn.

By the time the last week of school had arrived, I had thoroughly made up my mind. I was going home—back to Toronto. Maybe there my broken heart would have a chance to mend. In the evenings I packed my trunks; in went my books, my clothing, the china teapot, the knick-knacks, and the simple masterpieces presented to me by the children—"to teacher with love." I even packed my footstool, though why I kept it I couldn't be sure. I was certain that Mother wouldn't welcome the thing in the house.

Each item that I packed brought back memories, and when I came to the fur mittens, my gift from Wynn, I could endure no more. I threw myself on my lumpy bed and gave way to the luxury of tears. I loved this country—its bright, cloudless, blue, blue sky; the scent of roses in the air; the long, lingering twilight; even the wail of the cowardly coyotes. I loved the people—Anna with her hands that always held out some gift; Else with her shy eagerness; Mr. Dickerson with his desire that the community people be led in worship; Mr. Laverly who fought for a school even though his own sons were past school age; the Clarks, the Mattochs, Delaneys, Pastachucks, Thebeaus, and Blakes. They had become my neighbors, my people. Then I thought of dear, loving Andy and his honest praise for the efforts of his fellowman—"You did real good." The sobs shook my whole body.

I could have been so happy here, I mourned inwardly.

Then why run away? asked the other me.

I must—I must, was my only answer.

I went through the motions of teaching that last week. Each accomplishment of a student, each act of kindness raised a lump in my throat.

On the final day we had a picnic. Everyone from the community was there. I was flooded by kind and sincere compliments. It could have gone to my head had I been able to think clearly. Over and over again I heard the question, "Will you be back next fall, Miss Thatcher? Will you be our teacher again?" I could only reply in my dazed condition, "I don't know—I'm not sure."

Everyone seemed to enjoy the picnic, and as long as I kept busy I enjoyed it too. In the back of my mind the words kept hammering, *My last day—my last day.* I had to force my mind to other things so that I wouldn't succumb to the temptation to cry, right in front of them all.

It was time for them all to leave. My hand was shaken so often and so vigorously that it went numb—*as numb as my heart,* I thought, and then realized that my heart wasn't numb after all, for a sharp pain was twisting it.

I hugged my younger students and the older girls. Many of them cried, and I longed to cry with them. The boys stiffly shook hands in an embarrassed way, and even that touched me. At last the final wagon pulled away from the schoolyard, its occupants still waving and calling good-bye, and I turned back to the schoolroom. There really wasn't much that needed to be done, but I wanted to leave everything in good order. I swept, dusted, arranged, cleaned the blackboards, and scrubbed the floor. When everything was as clean as I could possibly make it, I took one last look around and, with tears in my eyes, went out and closed the door tightly behind me.

I spent the evening gathering and packing the last of my belongings and giving the teacherage a thorough cleaning as well. I was glad for every job that I found to do, for it kept my hands busy, if not my thoughts.

Just before retiring I went to my trunk and unpacked the china teapot and the two cups and saucers, wrapped them carefully, and placed them in a small box. Then I also pulled out the footstool. I looked at it long and lovingly, and then set it beside the door with the box.

The coyotes began their evening chorus. Their cries no longer frightened me; instead, they filled me with such a loneliness that I cried with them. *I may never hear them again,* I thought, and I knew that I would miss even them.

The next morning the whole Peterson family drove me to the station. I was so busy taking a good look at everything for the last time that I wasn't very good company. In fact, we were all rather quiet on that trip to Lacombe.

When we arrived at the station, Lars and Mr. Peterson checked my trunks while I purchased my ticket. We chatted in a rather empty fashion for a few minutes, and then it was time for me to go.

I hugged Anna warmly.

"I can never tell you how much your friendship and thoughtfulness have meant to me, and I have left something in the teacherage that I want you to have. You have given me so much and I've never given much in return." Anna protested, but I went on. "I want you to have my teapot, and I'd like Else and Olga to each have one of the cups and saucers to remember me by. And for Lars, for hauling wood and water and being such a good help to a green city girl, I have left my footstool—and for each of the children, one of my books. Lars always sat on the footstool when he read my books, so when he reads again, perhaps he can use the footstool and remember just how much this schoolteacher thought of him."

Then we all hugged some more and the whistle of the train announced that it would soon be leaving. I had to go. The train pulled away from the station with all of us still waving to one another.

I didn't cry *all* the way to Calgary. It was much too long a trip for that, but I did soak several lace handkerchiefs with my tears.

My day spent at Jon and Mary's was no better. They tried to convince me to stay, but I reminded them that my trunks were likely already on the way to Toronto. I was half-afraid that had I not taken the action of booking them to Toronto from Lacombe, I might have decided to stay. I couldn't do that. I just couldn't.

As Jon, Mary, and the children took me to the station the next day, we were all red-eyed. Kathleen clung to my hand.

"I wanted you to be my Aunt Beth for *always,"* she declared sadly.

"But I *am* your Aunt Beth for always."

"But I wanted you to be my Aunt Beth here."

I looked back at the hill where we had gone sledding. From the high rise above the hillside, one could look out over the Rocky Mountains. I had not made my promised trip to the mountain streams or steep slopes.

I'm coming back—someday, I silently promised. *I'm going to keep that promise if it's at all possible.*

Again there were tearful good-byes. I held each one of the family: the big brother that I had come to love and respect; Mary, my bright-haired new sister; William, the boy who would soon be a man; Sarah, with her shy, winning ways; Kathleen, the chattery, lovable bundle of energy; and Baby Elizabeth, a small bit of warmth and love who bore my name.

"I will miss you all so very much," I said through my tears.

Kathleen needed one last hug. "Come back, Aunt Beth—please come back soon." I promised to try, and then was making my way to the boarding platform, struggling with my tears.

"Elizabeth."

A hand was placed on my shoulder, and through the mist in my eyes I saw a red-coated chest and I looked up into the face of Wynn Delaney. His eyes looked troubled as they gazed deeply into mine.

"Elizabeth, I must see you."

"But my train—"

"I promise not to be long. There are still a few minutes."

His eyes seemed to plead and I could no longer bear to look at him. I lowered my gaze and nodded an agreement. He took my arm and steered me through the crowd and back into the station, while a confused redcap followed with my luggage.

"Dick," Wynn said to a man wearing a station man's uniform, "I need to borrow your office for a minute."

The man nodded. I was ushered into an office and the door closed behind me. Wynn turned me around to face him.

"Elizabeth," he said slowly, "I couldn't let you go this way. I've been miserable."

"Look, Wynn," I cut in rather hastily, "we were both wrong. It shouldn't have happened like that—but it did. You don't need to apologize."

I went to turn away from him and escape back to the train, but he held me firmly.

"Elizabeth, look at me."

Reluctantly I raised my eyes. My tears spilled over and ran down my cheeks.

"Elizabeth, I must confess that I kissed you because I *wanted* to—not merely to save you from fainting again. But I didn't come here just to apologize."

My eyes must have asked my question.

"I came here to ask you to forgive me, yes—but I also came to—to ask you not to go. I know it's selfish, and I know that I have no right, but I must at least tell you before you go—before you decide—that—I love you, Elizabeth. I want you to stay. I want you to consider being my wife. I know that I have nothing to offer—that I—"

I don't know what other nonsense Wynn might have gone on declaring had I not stopped him. I was still mulling over the words, "I love you, I want you to be my wife." And with a glad little cry I threw myself into his arms.

"Oh, Wynn!" I sobbed, and my tears spilled freely on his red tunic until he lifted my face upward and began to kiss me.

When he stopped and looked at me, I was breathless and flushed with happiness.

"I still don't know where I'll be posted—"

"It doesn't matter. Can't you see? It really doesn't matter."

"I believe you. Somehow I believe you." And he kissed me again.

The next question that he asked me made my eyes shine even more.

"How would you like a honeymoon in those Rockies—by a mountain stream?"

"Oh, Wynn, I'd love it. I'd just love it! Could we?"

Then a sharp train whistle reached my ears and even as I listened I could tell that it was getting farther away.

"Oh, dear," I said and looked at Wynn in dismay.

"What is it?"

"I do believe that my train has just left without me."

Wynn smiled his slow, deliberate smile. "Isn't that a shame," he said with exaggerated alarm.

Then I began to laugh—a soft, merry, tremendously happy laugh.

"Do you know," I said, "that my poor old trunks have gone on east without me?"

He pulled me close and laughed with me, kissing the top of my head.

"I do hope that you have *some* belongings, Elizabeth."

"Just my two suitcases."

"We'll wire ahead and have your trunks sent back—because I'm not letting you go after them. Trunks or no trunks, you're staying here—where you belong."

I had no objections.

Children's Books by Janette Oke

www.janetteoke.com

JANETTE OKE CLASSICS FOR GIRLS
(for girls ages 10–14)

The Bluebird and the Sparrow
The Calling of Emily Evans
Drums of Change
A Gown of Spanish Lace
Heart of the Wilderness
Roses for Mama

PICTURE BOOKS
(for all ages)

I Wonder... Did Jesus Have a Pet Lamb?

JANETTE OKE'S ANIMAL FRIENDS
(full-color, for young readers)

Spunky's Diary
The Prodigal Cat
The Impatient Turtle
This Little Pig
New Kid in Town
Ducktails
A Cote of Many Colors
A Prairie Dog Town
Maury Had a Little Lamb
Trouble in a Fur Coat
Pordy's Prickly Problem
Who's New at the Zoo?

04C

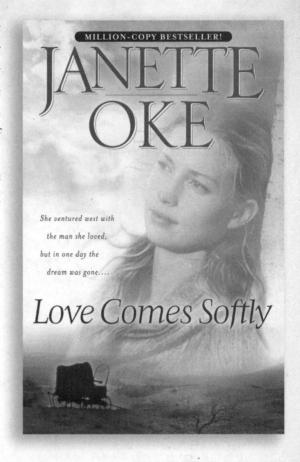

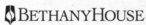